"IS THE TRUTH SO SCARY, ANABEL? WHY CAN'T YOU ACCEPT IT? WE BELONG TOGETHER."

She straightened, her eyes widening as she faced him. "No, you're wrong. We have *no* future together. Too much has happened. I don't blame you anymore for my brother's death. But don't you see, that doesn't change anything."

"But I said I love you. That must mean something to you."

"Jud, please don't . . ." She broke off as she watched his anger mount.

"Don't what?" he demanded. "Don't make you face the truth? That you haven't really forgiven me or yourself. That you're so stubborn you're harboring an eight-year-old resentment and want to waste the rest of your life—and mine—keeping it alive?"

CANDLELIGHT ECSTASY ROMANCES®

SECRET INTENTIONS

Jean Hager

Published by Dell Publishing Co., Inc.

Printed in the United States of America

A CANDLELIGHT ECSTASY ROMANCE®

Published by
Dell Publishing Co., Inc.
1 Dag Hammarskjold Plaza
New York, New York 10017

Dell ® TM 681510, Dell Publishing Co., Inc.

Candlelight Ecstasy Romance®, 1,203,540, is a registered
trademark of Dell Publishing Co., Inc., New York, New York.

ISBN: 0-440-17632-8

Printed in the United States of America

First printing—August 1985

To Our Readers:

We have been delighted with your enthusiastic response to Candlelight Ecstasy Romances®, and we thank you for the interest you have shown in this exciting series.

In the upcoming months we will continue to present the distinctive sensuous love stories you have come to expect only from Ecstasy. We look forward to bringing you many more books from your favorite authors and also the very finest work from new authors of contemporary romantic fiction.

As always, we are striving to present the unique, absorbing love stories that you enjoy most—books that are more than ordinary romance. Your suggestions and comments are always welcome. Please write to us at the address below.

Sincerely,

The Editors
Candlelight Romances
1 Dag Hammarskjold Plaza
New York, New York 10017

CHAPTER ONE

She had lived this horror before.

It was always raining.

The rain hurtled down in torrents. It thundered on the car's roof and windshield, sounding as though it would leave dents. She squinted her way through the sheets of water. Most of the time she couldn't see the sickly yellow glow from the streetlights, and the river was in a separate world. The rain overwhelmed the windshield wipers periodically, plunging her into a timeless, directionless universe. Crawling along Lockwood Drive, trying to give enough space to the few cars she passed, she fought panic, the desire to tromp the accelerator to the floor.

Beside her, Tim clutched his stomach and groaned. "How far, Anabel?"

She swallowed fear. "A block or two. Hang on, babe. We're almost there."

He twisted in the seat, his breath coming hard and fast. "It's worse, Anabel. Feels like my guts are being tied in knots. What's wrong with me?"

She glanced at her brother. Poised on the threshold of manhood, he was beautiful, golden, everything a young man should be. But now his face was contorted with pain. The eerie light from the dash illuminated beads of sweat on his forehead and upper lip. "Probably your appendix. They'll run tests to make sure."

"Will they operate?"

"Maybe. Don't worry about it. If they say surgery, we'll get Dr. Nesbett. He's the best." Even though it was Saturday night, she knew Nesbett would come at her request; she was a medical student, a member of the club.

She longed to smooth the damp blond hair off Tim's forehead, to tissue away the sweat with gentle, soothing strokes; but she didn't dare take her hands off the wheel.

She turned her attention to the street ahead, and that was when she saw the lights of an oncoming car. It was approaching far too fast on the slick street. Panic crawled back into her throat as she realized that the car was in her lane. For an instant she froze. Then she reacted with a convulsive jerk of the wheel. The oncoming car roared past, adding upward-moving curtains of water to those that dropped from the sky and preventing her from seeing anything through the windows.

She was driving blind! Her body clenched, expecting collision, crashing, oblivion. As though to underscore her intimation of disaster, lightning cracked and flashed, and thunder rumbled.

By the time the windshield wipers cleared a space

she could see through, feeble circles of light from the street lamps were rushing by. Unconsciously she had tread too hard on the accelerator. Reflexively she applied the brakes, and the car fishtailed and began to slide. She turned into the skid, her heart hammering as loudly in her ears as the rain pounding on the roof. She tapped the brake pedal once, twice, three times. Miraculously the car slowed and straightened out. She slumped back against the seat, perspiring now herself, as profusely as Tim.

The rain abated a bit. Ahead and to her right the shadowed marina appeared, telling her the medical center complex must be on her left. She searched for a street sign. There it was: Calhoun. She had passed the medical center, but she could reach it from Calhoun.

She turned left and Tim groaned. "We're almost there," she said. "You won't have to hurt much longer, Timmy." She hadn't called him Timmy since, at the age of twelve, he had demanded that she stop. It was a baby name, he'd said.

She pulled up to the emergency exit. "Be right back." She stepped out and into a puddle that was deep enough to cover her foot. She splashed toward the lighted double doors, water streaming from her head and down her back inside her dress, her shoes squishing, and a half-hysterical explanation ready to burst from her throat. Some part of her brain remained calm enough for her to register that professional detachment deserted when the patient was a loved one.

9

Seconds later the trauma team had brought Tim inside, and a sample of his blood had been rushed to the lab. She must have stood beside Tim in one of the curtained cubicles, holding his hand, smoothing his brow, murmuring comforts; but afterward her memory had lost that part.

The next thing she knew, Tim was being rushed to surgery. Because of her connection with the hospital, she was allowed to accompany him all the way to the doors leading to the surgical suites. Tim spoke only once as they wheeled him into the elevator. "I'm scared, Sis."

"Don't be. It's a routine procedure. Dr. Nesbett's done hundreds of appendectomies. Everything will be all right. I promise."

Before the surgery, Nesbett came out of the operating room to speak to her. "His white count's nineteen thousand, Anabel. If we don't operate, we run a high risk of rupture."

"I know."

"Jud's going to give the anesthetic."

"He's been on duty twenty-four hours straight. He must be exhausted."

"He caught a nap earlier. He's okay. Why don't you go find some coffee and try to rest?"

She nodded, gesturing toward the doctors' lounge next to the surgical suites. Her panic was dissipating; she had given Tim into Nesbett's competent hands. "I'll be in here."

She made a fresh pot of coffee and sat alone in the lounge in her damp clothes while the clock on the wall clicked off the minutes with incredible slowness. Later, when Nesbett and Jud entered the room, she knew instantly that something was wrong. Their faces were drawn, and it wasn't just from weariness. In Jud's eyes she saw shock and grief.

She came to her feet in slow motion, dreading, knowing. "What's wrong?" Jud crossed the room, tried to put his arm around her, but she shrugged it away. She looked at Nesbett, her eyes begging. "Tell me!"

"We couldn't . . . oh, damn, damn—" His voice broke. The unflappable Nesbett's professional manner cracked. "Anabel, I'm so sorry. He's gone."

Gone? Her beloved Tim, a prime specimen of young, healthy manhood, dead from an appendectomy? It wasn't possible. She couldn't accept it.

"No. No, please. *Please, no.*"

Nesbett and Jud exchanged desperate looks. Jud's fingers gripped her shoulder convulsively. "Anabel, I don't know how it happened. There was oxygen in the machine, but he wasn't getting any." The low, agonized words hung in the room like doom, heavy with the weight of their meaning.

She looked up at Jud, beginning to comprehend and not wanting to. Tears swam in his eyes. "I checked the machine before surgery, I swear it. It was ready to go when I stepped outside."

A trickle of understanding entered her mind, and she couldn't make it go away. He was talking about the anesthetic machine. Somehow the machine had failed. Jud had checked the machine. Jud was to blame. "You? You killed Tim?"

"Anabel!" Nesbett spoke sharply, sensing hysteria. "It happens. You know that. No one could have foreseen—"

"You . . ." All at once, full comprehension fell on her, filled her, exploded in her brain. She twisted away from Jud, stood with her feet spread, bracing herself, staring at the man she had thought she loved beyond all others. Wordlessly he lifted his hands to her in mute pleading.

"You killed him," she whispered. "You killed my Tim!" Suddenly the hands that reached out to her were covered with blood, dripping Tim's life force in scarlet circles on the floor.

"Anabel, please—"

"I'll never forgive you! Murderer!" So quickly, in the blink of an eye, can love turn to hate. Sobs racked her, seeming to tear her heart from her body. Gladly she would have given her own life for Tim's.

She bolted from the lounge, and time was altered, running backward. She stood beside the operating table and watched Tim's fine young body fight for air. He saw her, recognized her. "You said everything would be all right," he gasped. *You promised, Anabel!*" She tried with every ounce of her will and energy to touch him, to place her mouth on his and give him life; but she was paralyzed. She couldn't move a finger as she watched Tim draw his last breath.

Her sobs went on and on. . . .

Anabel shot from the bottom of sleep with the suddenness of a swimmer pursued by sharks. Anguish resided in her chest and clung to her skin like a spider's stringy web. She sat up in bed, her eyes searching the dark room for familiar shapes. The triple dresser was a hulking, dark mass against the wall to her right. The double windows in front of her were barely visible; fuzzy, gray rectangles. Fresh, cool air drifted to her from the open window. Rain drummed on the roof, not the deluge of her dream but a gentle, rhythmic patter.

She brushed her fingertips across her cheek. It was wet with tears. Slowly she came back to real time and place. Oriented at last, she used a corner of the sheet to dry her face and got up to close the window. The sill was wet; it glistened like glass in the light from the street. Her eyes more accustomed to the darkness now, she made her way to the bathroom without turning on any lights and brought back a towel to dry the sill.

She rested her forehead against the cool pane and looked down at the shadowy street. The neighborhood was one of old-fashioned, two-story brick homes. Most of them, like hers, had been lovingly restored with modern plumbing, heating, and cooling added. This was the historic section of Charleston known as the Battery. Anabel had fallen in love with the neighborhood on first sight and had promised herself, when she finished her training as an anesthesiologist, she would save enough money for a down payment on one of the gracious old homes.

She had lived frugally, despite her generous salary at the hospital. Four years later she had saved enough for the down payment and a start on the restoration. She had moved in, and the most needed restoration had been completed six months after that. The house was home, haven, and retreat from the problems of the workaday world.

But even the house couldn't shield her from the pain that was buried deep in her subconscious. She had thought it might; she hadn't had the dream since moving in a year ago. Until tonight.

The dream was the same mixture of reality and illusion that had haunted her sleep regularly in the past. In reality it had been raining that night, but she had driven Tim to the hospital without incident. The only blood on Jud's hands had been figurative. She had not seen Tim on the operating table or heard the accusing last words that always ended the dream. Some darkly creative corner of her mind had added the illusion to the reality.

She knew, of course, why the dream had come back to plague her tonight. Jud was returning to Charleston after eight years. Tomorrow he would be in the hospital. Tomorrow she might see him. She turned and read the luminous face of the bedside clock: four A.M. Not tomorrow, today.

She shivered, and rubbing her bare upper arms, she felt goose bumps. Was the reaction caused by the night chill or the knowledge that the years of reprieve had run out? April first had arrived. For the first time she was aware of the irony. April Fool's Day.

If she didn't see Jud today, she would see him one day very soon. No way to avoid it. "The best way around is always through," Lucy had said. She knew her friend was right, but knowing wouldn't make this day any easier.

There would be no more sleep for her tonight. Sighing, she drew the draperies and switched on the light. After putting on her robe and slippers, she descended the curving staircase, her hand gliding along the satiny mahogany banister. The stairway descended to a wide, tiled entrance hall with doors opening from it on four sides. She reversed her direction, taking the door that led to the kitchen and utility area. She would do the laundry, make tea, perhaps fix something for dinner that could be popped into the oven when she got home.

The rain tapered off to a fine drizzle that stopped shortly before six. She sat at her oak breakfast table and watched dawn turn the sky gradually from charcoal to dove-gray to pale blue. She enjoyed being alone. It hadn't been that way following Tim's death, but she'd worked her way through the worst of it, and now solitude was fine. As long as there wasn't too much of it.

She told herself she should get up and cook breakfast; but she found she couldn't make the effort. When she finally moved, it was to transfer the last load of laundry from washer to dryer. The tightness in her chest that had been there since she awoke had not left her entirely; and she suspected breakfast would not sit well on her stomach this morning. She went back upstairs to get ready for work.

Lucy Tremaine phoned at seven. Anabel had just stepped out of the shower when she heard the ringing, and she grabbed a towel to wrap around her as she ran to answer.

"Come to breakfast," Lucy said without preamble.

"It's sweet of you to think of me," Anabel said, "but I don't—"

"Don't say no until you hear the menu. Fresh country eggs. Canadian bacon. Honeydew melon. Huge, fresh strawberries."

Anabel was laughing. "Nobody could turn that down. What's gotten into you? I seem to remember Bill saying you usually have cereal on weekdays."

"So I feel like fussing. Put it down to spring fever. Can you be here in twenty minutes?"

"I'll do my best."

Anabel dried her hair and put it up, then dressed hastily in a tailored navy skirt and blouse. Still not sure she could eat much, nevertheless she would try. She knew Lucy's unprecedented breakfast invitation was no casual impulse. Lucy knew Jud was scheduled to arrive at the hospital today. Preparing a lavish breakfast was her way of fortifying her friend for the ordeal.

The least Anabel could do was pretend to have an appetite. She owed Lucy Tremaine more than she could ever repay. If it hadn't been for Lucy, Anabel wasn't sure she would have made it through those

16

first months following Tim's death. She had wanted to drop out of medical school and crawl away somewhere to die. Lucy wouldn't hear of it.

"You have to keep busy," Lucy had said. "Work until you drop. That's the only way to get over what's happened."

Anabel couldn't count the nights Lucy had left her husband alone to stay with Anabel when she couldn't sleep. Through some sixth sense Lucy always seemed to know when Anabel was having one of those nights. She would appear without notice, carrying a bag of needlework. She would make a pot of tea, sit Anabel down, take out her knitting or crocheting, and talk. My, how they did talk! Into the wee hours when, exhausted, Anabel couldn't hold her eyes open any longer. When she awoke the next morning, Lucy would be gone.

It was odd, considering that Lucy was ten years older than Anabel, how close the two women had become. Eight years ago Lucy had been a nurse at the hospital. Most of the time she had circulated in surgery. In fact, she had been called back on an emergency operation the night Tim died; the surgery had been performed in the same operating room before Tim was brought in. So Lucy had gone home without knowing of the tragic death of seventeen-year-old Tim Dixon until the next day.

She had gone to Anabel's apartment immediately after hearing the news, and she had stayed a week, helping Anabel cope with the funeral arrangements and disposing of Tim's things. At the end of the week

17

Lucy had started her campaign to get Anabel back into her regular routine. "Listen to me, Anabel," she said. "It's impossible to think about two things at the same time. You can't deny that. While you're concentrating in class or working at the hospital, you won't think of Tim." Lucy and her irrefutable arguments that had sent Anabel back to school.

Little more than casual acquaintances before, the two women discovered in the weeks following Tim's death a rare rapport. For the past eight years Lucy and Bill Tremaine had been Anabel's closest friends. They had become the nearest thing she had to a family.

The Tremaines lived in a modern town house in a row of similar homes a few blocks from South Battery. When Anabel arrived, Bill, in his working uniform, was leaving for his job as captain of one of the big boats that carried tourists on tours of the Charleston harbor and outlying forts.

At the front door he gave Anabel a brotherly peck on the cheek. "I'll be thinking about you today. Go get 'em, tiger."

She grinned. "Thanks, Bill. How's our favorite lady this morning?"

"The good Lord continues to smile on us," Bill said, settling his billed captain's cap on his sandy hair. "She's bursting with energy."

"Wonderful."

For the past year Lucy had been having heart problems. No longer employed at the hospital, she worked as a private duty nurse when she felt up to it.

18

When Lucy had a bad day, Anabel worried about her as deeply as Bill did. At those times she couldn't help thinking: All the people I love die. First her parents, then Tim. Or they betrayed her, like Jud, who had been ruthlessly excised from her life, like a malignant growth.

When each of the people she loved had left her, a piece of herself was torn away. When she let herself think about it, she wondered if she was strong enough to survive another such loss. Mostly she didn't let herself think about losing Lucy. She was so emotionally dependent on her friend that it terrified her to contemplate a life without Lucy's staunch, sensible presence.

Lucy had been feeling fine for the past several weeks, and Anabel gave silent thanks for that as she walked through the comfortable house to the gleaming red-and-white kitchen.

"Hey, where's my breakfast?" she called.

"In the oven. You're five minutes late."

Anabel checked her watch. "Oops. Sorry about that." She stood at the kitchen door and watched Lucy bustle from stove to table to refrigerator like a small, bright bird trying to fill the constantly open mouths in her nest. Lucy was a short, wiry woman who threw off sparks of energy like an electrified coil. Her brown hair was cut short and curled all over her head in the minimum-care style that Lucy preferred. Freckles were splattered across her short nose, and she rarely bothered to cover them with makeup, claiming she had better things to do than worry about hair and cosmetics. She was wearing a kelly-green cotton dress piped in white, with a starched white apron tied around her waist. As usual, when at home, she wore her favorite pair of worn, floppy scuffs.

Lucy removed two plates containing over-easy eggs and Canadian bacon from the oven and placed them on the table. As the two women sat down Lucy's green eyes scanned Anabel's silver-gilt hair, which was worn pulled away from her face and confined in a thick braid coiled at the back of her head. The fine, patrician features were unadorned except for a dusting of powder and delicate coral lip color. Her gaze settling on the dark lines beneath Anabel's silver-gray eyes, Lucy nodded as if a suspicion had been confirmed. "Bad night, huh?"

Anabel shrugged. "Short."

Lucy took a sip of coffee from a steaming cup. "How long have you been up?"

"Since four." Anabel's admission was accompanied by an apologetic look. There were times when Lucy's common sense, head-on approach to things filled her with feelings of inadequacy that dismayed her.

Lucy's thin brows rose. "Are you scheduled in surgery today?"

"No, thank goodness. I'll be in committee meetings and the office most of the day."

Lucy seemed to relax at this news. She offered Anabel a hot biscuit before selecting one and splitting it to add butter. "So, the famous Dr. Judson A.

Westby hits town today." Avoiding touchy subjects wasn't Lucy's style.

"I think I read something about that in the news-paper."

Lucy chuckled. Since Jud had agreed to move to Charleston, the newspapers had run several articles lauding his accomplishments and listing the honors bestowed on him as one of the South's renowned cardiovascular surgeons. It was rumored that the Charleston hospital where Anabel practiced had lured him away from Atlanta with guarantees of an astronomical salary plus lavish perks. "I heard Atlanta offered him the moon on a silver platter if he would stay."

Anabel concentrated on cutting her bacon. "Too bad they didn't have their way."

"It's really kind of odd."

"What is?"

"Atlanta's bigger than Charleston, and the hospital there must be twice as large. Makes you wonder why Jud would leave that to come here, doesn't it?"

"I haven't thought about it, Lucy. I try not to think about Jud at all if I can help it."

"It's going to be pretty hard to avoid it now."

"No. I may have to work with him occasionally, but he'll be just another surgeon as far as I'm concerned."

Lucy eyed her dryly. "Sounds sensible. How come I don't believe it? Ah, I know why. You couldn't sleep last night."

Anabel sighed. "I had the dream again."

"Oh, honey, I'm sorry. I was hoping you'd gotten through that."

"Me too. It's been a year." Anabel ate a few bites of her eggs and bacon, then put her fork down. She settled back to nibble at a strawberry and sip coffee.

"Jud's return is bound to be traumatic for you. Maybe the dream won't come again. I mean, once you've seen him, maybe you'll realize you can handle having him around."

"I devoutly hope so." Anabel toyed with a chunk of melon with the tip of her spoon. "If I only knew the answers to a few questions, I think I could put it all behind me."

Lucy made a sympathetic sound. "Like where did he go when he left Charleston? Why did he decide to leave anesthesiology and go into surgery?"

"I know why he left anesthesiology," Anabel said bitterly. "He killed Tim, and he couldn't handle the guilt."

"Now, Anabel," Lucy said patiently, "Jud always swore he checked that machine and it was in perfect working order."

Anabel's eyes flashed contemptuously. "Nonetheless, Tim got straight nitrous oxide, didn't he? The oxygen switch was *off*, Lucy."

"Jud was so sure, though. I know he'd been on duty for twenty-four hours, and he was tired—"

"He should have asked to be relieved," snapped Anabel, "but then Jud always did think he was super-human."

"Honey, you mustn't hate him for the rest of your life. It's not good for you."

"It's not a question of must or mustn't. It's that I *can't* forgive him, ever."

"He's a skilled cardiovascular surgeon now. He's saved so many lives. Can't you try to separate the Jud you knew—the Jud who made one terrible, fatal, human mistake—from the Jud today?"

"I don't know, Lucy. That one mistake cost my brother's life. I've tried to picture Jud eight years older, picture the two of us working together, relaxed with each other. But I can't even imagine him doing open-heart surgery. Of course, I'll be forced to watch him soon enough. Maybe then I'll believe it. But as for feeling comfortable with him—" She shook her head.

"You wouldn't . . ." Lucy hesitated, then blurted, "You aren't thinking of moving, are you?"

"Leave you and Bill, my beautiful house, Charleston? No way. I won't run away, Lucy. I won't let Jud drive me from the place and people I love."

Lucy cocked her head and reached across the table to give Anabel's hand a fond squeeze. "Good. After a few weeks you'll get used to seeing Jud at the hospital. It'll get easier every day, you'll see."

Anabel managed a lackluster laugh. "Ever the eternal optimist, aren't you? Well, maybe you're right. It certainly can't get worse."

"True."

"And you've done your part." Anabel's gaze swept the table. "You've fortified me with a fantastic breakfast and given me sensible advice. What would I do without you, friend?"

Lucy ducked her head in uncharacteristic embarrassment. She jumped up from the table and went to the counter for the coffeepot. As Bill had said, Lucy was full of energy this morning, but it seemed to Anabel that it was caused by an underlying frenetic tension. Lucy's face was flushed, and Anabel had the feeling Lucy couldn't meet her eyes for a moment. Funny how giving people frequently found it difficult to accept anything for themselves, even compliments. It was as if they couldn't tolerate having attention drawn to themselves. They were only comfortable lavishing attention on others.

Carrying the coffeepot, Lucy returned to the table. The flush was gone. She had recovered herself. "What are friends for?"

Anabel put her hand over her cup. "No more. I'm sloshing, as it is. Anyway, I have to go." She rose and, on impulse, hugged Lucy. At five feet seven inches, Anabel stood a half-foot taller than her friend. She held Lucy away from her for a close-up, critical look. Did she imagine it or was there the faintest blue tinge to Lucy's skin tone? "You planning to take it easy today?"

Lucy glided away from Anabel. "Don't fuss over me. You sound just like Bill."

Anabel watched Lucy's quick, nervous movements as she cleared the table. "Can we help it if we care about you?"

"Try smother."

24

Lucy's irritated tone puzzled Anabel. "Sorry." She glanced at her watch and saw that it was ten to eight. "I really have to go, Lucy."

Lucy turned from the sink and flashed a smile, her irritation gone as quickly as it had come. "So go. Go."

"Okay. Thanks for breakfast. And you lie down for a while this afternoon. That's an order."

"Yes, Doctor," said Lucy wryly.

Outside, Anabel stepped into her burgundy Buick. Lucy was a nurse, she reminded herself. She knew how to take care of herself.

Anabel drove the short distance to Lockwood Drive where she turned right. Ahead, the hospital towers rose against the pure blue sky. It was a new experience, approaching that building with dread. Within an hour or two Jud would be inside those walls. She drew in a deep, bracing breath. It was going to be a long and stressful day.

CHAPTER TWO

Gretchen Gorman, the secretary-receptionist who worked for the four anesthesiologists in Anabel's group, set a cup of steaming bouillon in front of Anabel. "Try this. You've already had too much coffee this morning."

Anabel pushed her reading glasses to the top of her head and stretched her neck and shoulders, trying to work out the kinks. "Is it break time already?"

"Yep. Ten-thirty." Gretchen, who never drank coffee, perched on a corner of Anabel's desk and blew on her bouillon. She was tall with long black hair, once a model who had done a lot of local fashion shows. Twice-divorced, the mother of two sons, she was a self-styled liberated woman who had laid down the law to her male bosses on her first day in the office: "I don't make, order, or serve food or drink during office hours. I don't shop for gifts for wives, mothers, daughters, or sweethearts. I won't take the responsibility of remembering anniversaries and birthdays for you. Any questions?" Sam Adler, at fifty-six the suave senior partner, had looked up and down Gretchen's long length and said, "Maybe you'd better tell us exactly what you will do, Ms. Gorman." Without a second's hesitation Gretchen had shot back, "I'll be the best secretary you ever had, Doctor." The following months proved that she hadn't exaggerated.

Gretchen usually brought Anabel something to drink when she went for her midmorning bouillon, however, presumably because Anabel never asked and because they were the only females in the office. Anabel admired the gutsy secretary, who was so different from herself, and a comfortable office friendship had developed between them.

Long-legged, wearing spike heels and a wildly swirling skirt and vest, black hair tumbling, green eyes outlined in exotic kohl, Gretchen looked like an advertisement for a tour of Italian wine festivals. "It's ten-thirty, Doc," she said, her voice deep and melodious. "You haven't looked up from that desk since eight. Like my mother used to tell me, you're gonna put your eyes out if you don't quit reading so much. Whyn't you go outside and play for a change."

Anabel sat back in her chair. "Somehow I can't picture you as a studious youngster, Gretchen."

Gretchen's spike-heeled foot was swinging. "Mom just thought I was studying. Behind an English literature book cover, I was reading sexy novels and fashion magazines. She never could figure out why my grades weren't any better. Poor Mom, she was so gullible."

Anabel grinned. "I'll bet your boys don't get away with a thing."

"Wrong," Gretchen announced. "I surprise myself sometimes. The other day I found a girlie magazine at the bottom of my thirteen-year-old's underwear drawer."

"What'd you do?"

"Put it back. Darrin doesn't even know I found it. If I told him, I'd have to confiscate the thing, and I don't want to spoil the fun of poring over the forbidden with a flashlight and the sheet pulled over his head. Every time I think of him sweating under there, I laugh."

"I'm amazed," Anabel said with a shake of her head. "No lecture on viewing women as sex objects?"

Gretchen lifted one shoulder and sipped her bouillon loudly. "You know I thought about it, but I decided he's not ready for the lecture yet. He has to go through this stage first."

"You're a wise woman, Gretch."

Gretchen lifted her Styrofoam cup as if to toast herself. "You think so? Then how about taking my advice. Finish up here and go out and find a man to play with."

"Last week you were off men."

"I can only hack despising all men for a week at a time. This week I'm willing to concede that there might conceivably be—somewhere out there—a wonderful, understanding man who sees women as real people with human needs and intelligence equal to his. And to put icing on the cake, he's fantastic in

28

bed. I thought I found him twice and was fooled but, hey, you have to kiss a lot of frogs to find a prince. Now be honest with me, wouldn't you like to chuck all these boring medical records and go find your prince?"

"Oh, Gretchen, where would I start? No, I'm too old for chasing rainbows."

"Thirty-three is not around the bend, kiddo. Look at me. I'm thirty-seven and just entering my prime." She rose and, holding her cup out, spun on her heels, sending fringes, layers, gold chains, and black hair flying.

Anabel leaned back in her chair, enjoying her bouillon and laughing. "I guess it's just a difference in point of view."

"Is that a nice way of telling me to grow up?" Gretchen asked, flopping down on the desk again. "No, don't answer that. You're always so mature and sensible, and I'm always vacillating between Mean Mama and Cindy at the Prom." She grinned, confident enough to poke fun at herself, such an experienced woman of the world. She sighed. "At least, no man has ever accused me of being predictable. Other things, sure. My last husband said I was an exhibitionist. That was after I wore a dress with a neckline veed to the waist to his parents' house for dinner. Tony and his mother sulked like two old spayed bulldogs all evening. His dad and I had a good time, though."

Anabel was laughing so hard, she had to set her

bouillon down to keep from spilling it. "Oh, Gretch, you're wonderful," she said with a gasp.

"Listen, I know it and you know it, but how are we gonna get the message to the world? On second thought, forget the world. I'd settle for getting the message to one man. Dr. Westby."

Anabel's laugh was cut off abruptly. "Who?"

"Judson A. Westby. You know, the big heart doc everybody's so excited about."

"Have you seen him?"

"Just a glimpse but enough. Mercy, what a man."

"In the hospital? This morning?"

Gretchen eyed Anabel curiously. "Sure. When I went to the snack shop to get the bouillon. Dr. Westby walked by with two other surgeons. I heard one of them call him Jud, but I'd have recognized him from his pictures in the newspaper. I tell you, he could be a prince. He's definitely got possibilities." She batted her false eyelashes wickedly. "Of course, I'd have to kiss him to be sure."

"Did you hear what they were talking about?"

"Going to the country club for lunch, I think." Thoughtfully Gretchen pursed her lips. "Uh, why are you interested?"

Why, indeed. The tension of wondering at what moment she would come face-to-face with Jud was getting to her. In fact, she had been hiding in the office all morning, putting off the inevitable. Gretchen would never understand that. Gretchen would hunt Jud down, deal with seeing him again, get it over with.

30

"I'm not really."

"You could have fooled me. Do you know Westby?"

"No," Anabel said too quickly. "I mean, I used to, a long time ago."

"Oh." Gretchen's eyes lit up. *"Oh."*

Anabel gazed into her bouillon.

"I don't know what he did, but he sure made an impression on you."

Anabel never learned what else Gretchen might have said. At that moment somebody entered the outer office, and Gretchen went back to her desk.

Listening to the conversation in the outer office, Anabel recognized the voice of Leroy Sandifer, head of the hospital business office. Sandifer was a small, proper man in his fifties who had never been married and lived with his mother.

She heard Gretchen ask, "New suit, Sandy?" Nobody but Gretchen called him Sandy. It irritated him, which, of course, was why Gretchen did it.

"Yes," Sandifer answered tersely. "Why are you staring at me like that?"

"I've never seen you wear a pink shirt before," Gretchen said. "Goes well with the suit, though."

"Do you think it's too loud?" Sandifer sounded worried.

"Not at all. It's . . . well, there's only one word for it, Sandy. It's precious."

Anabel choked back a laugh as she pictured Leroy Sandifer, his face red with indignation. Poor man. He simply was no match for Gretch.

Sandifer sniffed. "The man at the store assured me

31

colored shirts are in this year. Besides, who are you to cast stones? The way you dress . . . well, you're certainly not my idea of a secretary."

"Gee, Sandy, I guess I'll just have to live with that."

Leroy said petulantly, "If I had my way, you wouldn't be able to talk that way to your superiors."

"Aw, come on, Sandy, let's be friends."

There was a small silence while Leroy tried to decide if this was just another one of Gretchen's perverse jokes. Finally he decided to ignore it. "Is Dr. Adler in?"

Anabel returned her attention to the medical records as she heard Gretchen saying that the senior partner wouldn't be in the office until after lunch. With an enormous effort she pushed to the back of her mind the information that Jud was in the hospital and concentrated on the business at hand.

At eleven forty-five Gretchen buzzed her to say that Mason Kelsey was on the line. Mason, one of the hospital's three assistant administrators, had escorted Anabel to several hospital-related social functions. He was about her age, red-haired and freckled, and she liked him. She lifted the receiver.

"Hi, Mason."

"Hi. Are you busy?"

"Aren't I always? Why do you ask?"

"Thought you might meet me for lunch in the cafeteria. We haven't had a chance to talk in weeks."

"I know." She had planned to skip lunch and keep to the safety of her office until time for the afternoon committee meeting in the boardroom. But since

Gretchen had heard Jud and two other doctors making plans for lunch at the country club, Anabel knew she wouldn't run into Jud in the cafeteria. "I'd like to have lunch with you, Mason. What time?"

"Twelve-fifteen okay?"

"Fine. See you then."

A few minutes later, as she was leaving the office, she told Gretchen, "If you need me, I'll be lunching with Mason Kelsey in the cafeteria."

Gretchen, who was filing copies of the morning's correspondence, leaned an elbow on the file cabinet. "He's not your prince," she observed matter-of-factly.

"I know it, but he's sweet."

Gretchen rolled her eyes. "The kiss of death."

As she waited for the elevator Anabel thought about what Gretchen had said, reflecting that her lack of emotional involvement with Mason was precisely why she felt so at ease with him. They were friends, and for Anabel, it could never go beyond that. Since she knew that Mason, whose boyish grin made many female hearts flutter, occasionally dated other women, she took it for granted that his perception of their relationship was the same as hers.

Mason had reached the cafeteria before her and was saving her a place in line. Of medium height and muscular, Mason looked quite smashing in a dark blue suit. The line moved quickly, and a few minutes later they were seated at a table in a room reserved for physicians and administrative staff—the VIP lunchroom, as it was called by other hospital employees.

"You look tired," Mason said. "Are you working too hard?"

"No harder than usual. I just didn't sleep well last night."

He watched her stir cream into her coffee, her face turned in profile, head bent, exposing the lines of her elegant, slender neck. It was Mason's habit to study the lovely Dr. Anabel Dixon when she was absorbed in something and unaware of his perusal. Knowing that she regarded him as merely a friend, he saw other women frequently. There were times, particularly after an evening with Anabel had left him frustrated, when he wished he could fall in love with one of the willing women he regularly took to bed. But it hadn't happened because, he suspected, he continued to be intrigued by Anabel. She was extremely intelligent and quite attractive, even though she seemed determined to hide her physical beauty with severe hairstyles and an absence of makeup. He was discovering that she had a quick wit when she felt at ease, and Mason had worked hard at making her feel at ease with him; but even though she had progressed to feeling comfortable with him, in the six months since he had escorted her to an employee awards banquet, she was still the most private person he had ever known. She could relax with him now, yet she remained a stranger to him on all but the most superficial levels. This both fascinated and frustrated him.

She looked up at him quickly and smiled. Caught in the act of staring at her, he dropped his gaze and began to cut his meat loaf. They ate in companionable silence for several moments.

Finally he inquired, "Any particular reason for the sleepless night?"

She hesitated briefly before answering. "I suppose there's always a reason but nothing I could put my finger on. I'll make it up by getting to bed early tonight."

"I hope that doesn't mean you're not going to the reception for Dr. Westby." He gave her one of his engaging, boyish smiles.

Her eyes widened, and she put down her fork. "What reception?"

"The one the hospital's giving at the Sheraton. All employees were sent personal invitations. Didn't you get yours?"

"I suppose I must have." She remembered now. She had found the envelope in her mailbox two weeks ago. The invitation had been engraved on beige parchment, very chic. She had carried it immediately into her kitchen and dropped it in the wastebasket, made up her mind to forget it.

He watched as she picked up her knife and buttered a roll. "Well, are you going?"

"I'd forgotten," she said. "I'm really not in the mood for a reception, Mason. I think I'll skip it."

"Skip it?" He couldn't keep his surprise out of his voice. "If you do, you'll be the only hospital employee who does. Everybody's eaten up by curiosity,

35

and they won't miss the chance to meet Westby. His work has received so much publicity, he's practically a celebrity. Aren't you the least bit curious about him?"

She shook her head. "Not really." But she didn't meet his eyes.

He would never understand her, he thought. He chose his words carefully. "It's sort of a command performance, Anabel. All the members of the board will be there. Your absence might be noted."

Her chin came up. Her gray eyes narrowed. "A command performance? That's ridiculous, Mason."

"Maybe I should explain to you how the board feels about having such a distinguished surgeon on staff. Westby's decision to come here is a compliment and an honor for the hospital. When they made the offer, I don't think anyone expected it to be accepted. Nobody's quite sure why it was. We're grateful, of course, and I doubt that anyone will ever ask Westby for his reasons. Better not to look a gift horse in the mouth."

"Gift horse?" she echoed with what sounded to Mason like deliberate obtuseness.

"You know what I mean. Because of Westby, we'll be receiving national publicity. Gifts and grants we wouldn't have had a chance of receiving without him will come our way."

"All of which has nothing to do with me," Anabel snapped. "To tell you the truth I'm pretty sick of all the hullabaloo over the great Dr. Westby. He's a fallible human being, for heaven's sake, not a god."

Astonishingly she was angry. He'd never seen her angry before. If she had been any other doctor, Mason would have said it was anger rooted in envy. But sour grapes wasn't Anabel's style. He was totally baffled by her reaction and didn't know how to respond. Evidently he'd caught her on a bad day. Thinking that lunch hadn't been such a good idea after all, he returned to eating in silence and, after a moment, so did she.

His instincts told him to let the matter drop, but when she rose to return to her office, her lunch half-eaten, he couldn't keep from saying, "I was looking forward to escorting you to the reception. Don't you think you'll regret it later if you don't put in an appearance? We wouldn't have to stay long. Think about it, Anabel, and call me if you change your mind. I'll be home till seven-thirty."

After a long, tiring meeting of the surgical review committee, Anabel left the hospital at five-thirty. She walked to the employee parking garage, thinking about the problems posed by the increase in the number of the hospital's surgical procedures over the past quarter. A surgical schedule that was considered fair by all the hospital surgeons was becoming more and more difficult to organize. Henceforth the task would be performed by computer. That would, at least, take the pressure off nurses, who could now say to irate doctors, "Take it up with the computer."

She reached her car and fished the keys out of her purse.

"Anabel."

The voice came from the shadows in the near corner of the garage. It was low but oddly commanding nevertheless, and she would have known it anywhere. She couldn't pretend she hadn't heard because they would both know it was a pretense. She swiped a wisp of hair out of her eyes in a resigned gesture and turned around. He left the shadows and walked to the rear of her car. No more than six feet separated them.

"Jud," she said tonelessly.

It was amazing that her voice held no feeling when inside she was beset by a storm of emotions. She didn't know what she had expected, but what she had not expected was that he would look the same, this tall, lean man whom she hadn't seen in eight years, had never wanted to see again. It took several moments for the resentment to subside enough for her to detect the small differences: a sprinkling of gray in the wavy, brown hair; fans of fine lines at the outer corners of his eyes; an expression in those eyes that had not been there eight years ago—an odd mixture of sadness coupled with stoic calm.

He leaned a hip against the car trunk, careless of the thin film of dust being ground into his expensive suit. "I kept expecting to see you all day."

"I was busy," she retorted.

He lifted a brow. "Avoiding me, Anabel?"

"Maybe," she agreed.

His eyes narrowed. "We'll be working together."

"Not any more than I have to."

For a moment they stood measuring each other in silence. Behind Jud three nurses walked by, laughing. A faint breeze found its way into the open garage, stirring the dust. "Okay," Jud said at length, "I guess I expected that attitude."

She looked at him scornfully and started to open the car door. Jud took two steps and caught her arm. "It's not very professional," he added.

Anabel stiffened. She stared at the hand on her arm for a long moment before she raised her eyes to his. "Take your hand off me." Her lips hardly moved, and the words were said in a monotone of rigid control. But it was the ice in her gray eyes that prompted him to release her instantly.

To hide the tremor in his hand, he stuffed it in his trousers pocket. "You're going to have to deal with me sooner or later."

It seemed to her there was more in the blunt statement than he had put into words: *I have influence with the board. I can have and do whatever I want at the hospital. Take it or leave it.* Hot anger seared through her. "Why did you come back?" she blurted.

He eyed her calmly. "I had to." A simple statement of fact that explained nothing.

Anabel stared at him, warning herself to stop feeling anything until later. "I don't want to be in the same town with you."

"I know."

She could no longer think about anything but getting away. She got into the car and slammed the door. Shaken, she gripped the steering wheel fiercely for an instant, determined not to look back at him. Her pulse hammered at every point in her body. Because she was trembling, her movements were made with deliberate care as she started the engine and backed slowly out of the parking space.

Jud watched her drive away, his feet spread in a bracing stance to combat the quiver in his knees. He stood that way for several moments after she was gone, until he found his control.

She still blamed him. He had seen it in every rigid line of her body. Ruthlessly he quelled a surge of pain. Had he really expected anything else? Finally sadness took the place of the pain. In the stranger who had just driven away there was nothing of the carefree, vivacious girl he had known. Her movements had been tightly controlled, robotlike. Even her words had sounded planned and stilted, except for that brief outburst at the end of their conversation. All the spontaneity had been crushed out of her. It was almost as though she had died with Tim and someone else inhabited her body.

In control again, Jud strode to his silver-gray Mercedes, trying not to notice that the color reminded him of Anabel's eyes. He left the parking garage and drove toward the furnished suburban house he had rented for six months while the owners were out of the country. It was the home of strangers with its family photographs and quaint knickknacks that held

40

no meaning for him. No memories. That's the way he wanted it.

He planned to spend most of his time at the hospital, anyway.

CHAPTER THREE

The house had a closed-up smell. Airless. After turning on the air conditioning, Jud stripped off his jacket and loosened his tie. In the wet bar off the kitchen he made a martini, then carried it into the living room.

Weary, he sprawled on the floral print sofa. There were flowers everywhere in this house. Chosen, he supposed, to simulate a joyous, springtime environment. If so, he was unaffected; he wondered why anyone would want so many fake flowers, of so many varieties and colors, everywhere he looked. It was too much. It could get nauseating. Thank God he wouldn't be here much. He stared at a huge spray of red-and-pink roses on the sofa and felt depressed. But to be fair, it wasn't the flowers that depressed him.

Ah, Anabel . . .

Nursing the martini, he closed his eyes, remembering the Anabel of eight years ago. Being back at the hospital today had stirred memories he'd believed long since dead. He had met her during the last year of his anesthesiology residency. A senior medical student, she arrived at the hospital with several other students to pursue a three-month practicum that would introduce them to various medical specialties. The students were assigned to senior residents in each of the departments they had chosen. When Anabel rotated into anesthesiology, she was assigned to Jud.

She walked into his office that first day, and his life changed. Working too many hours, getting too little sleep, for three years his whole existence had been the hospital. Residencies were hell. He'd known that before he started, accepted it. Maybe he'd even reveled in it—in proving that he could take the grueling work schedule without allowing it to affect his performance. He was determined to be the best anesthesiologist in the country.

Then Anabel entered his life, bringing beauty and fun at a time when he had almost forgotten that beauty and fun existed. He hardly remembered how to laugh until she taught him again. At twenty-five she had seemed and looked younger, so fresh and open and giving. He'd been amazed to learn, in her second week in his department, that she was raising a teenage brother alone. Beneath her seeming naïveté, there was a compassionate, responsible woman. Jud became more intrigued by her every day.

At the end of the third week he had a rare weekend night free and asked her to have dinner with him.

She had flashed him a pleased smile. "Why, Dr.

Westby, I didn't think you even knew my name. I'd love to have dinner with you."

On the way to pick her up that evening, he'd felt a stirring of excitement. Excitement that had nothing to do with medicine. It had been years since he'd experienced anything quite like it. Oh, there had been a few women during the past three years. Warm bodies to satisfy elemental needs, women who made not even a ripple of impression on the surface of his life. During the few hours he spent with such women now and then, he almost resented the physical hungers that diverted him from his obsessive pursuit of professional goals, even if briefly. Afterward he sometimes found it difficult to remember what they looked like.

But something different was happening with Anabel. He kept seeing her face and hearing her voice while he was shaving or driving to and from the hospital. Twice he awoke in the night to find himself reaching for her, dreaming that she was all soft and warmly naked next to him in bed. Both times his body had ached painfully for a long time afterward.

During dinner, her lovely face somber, she had spoken of her parents, who had died during the past year. Then, smiling again, she'd told him about her seventeen-year-old brother, Tim.

"It must be hard on you," he said, "raising a teenage boy while going to medical school."

She looked surprised. "Oh, no, it's not hard at all—except for a rather tight budget. Tim's the only family I have left, and he's the greatest joy in my life."

44

She laughed softly. "I realize I'm prejudiced, but Tim is really an extraordinary kid. He's mature for his age and handsome and bright." She paused a moment, then went on unabashed. "He's considerate too. He does more of the housework than I do. I'm going to miss him terribly when he goes to college next year."

She was easy to talk to. They talked all evening, and he laughed more than he could ever remember doing. It wasn't that their conversation was particularly witty; it was simply that being with her made him happy. On her front porch, when he took her home, he planted his hands firmly at her waist and pulled her to him. He stood, looking down at her. Light from the naked bulb over the door showered on her hair, streaking it with pale, undulating flames and silvering the strands that fell forward across her shoulders.

A smile hovered on her lips, and she sounded breathless as she said, with an honesty that pleased and humbled him, "You make my knees tremble when you touch me."

He laughed, a low rumble. "Why do you think I'm holding on to you? I'm not exactly as steady as a rock myself."

There was mischief in her eyes, and she lifted a pale brow. "Is that the only reason you're holding on to me?" Her sweet breath touched his lips.

He lifted a hand, and his eyes continued to hold hers as he tangled his fingers in her hair. "Huh-uh."

He cupped his hand around the base of her neck.

She let out a quiet, shaky breath. "I didn't think so." She sighed as his mouth closed over hers.

The kiss began as a light good night. At least, that's what he thought he intended. Perhaps if she hadn't relaxed so completely, leaning against him, if she hadn't felt so warm and pliant in his arms, if her breasts hadn't pressed softly but insistently against his chest, it would have stopped at a mere brush of lips.

But as their mouths met, her lips parted invitingly, and he tasted the moist tip of her tongue. His heart lurched and, for an incredible moment, seemed to stop pumping. Then, with a delayed, fierce throb, his blood surged and swam wildly. And there was no lightness in the kiss anymore.

Hot and yearning, their mouths feasted on the depths of each other, moist and endlessly hungry. At the back of his throat a groan of pleasure was muffled as he took the kiss deeper still, exploring the taste and texture of her teeth and tongue and the intimacy of her mouth. The flavor and feel and scent of her overwhelmed and intoxicated him. He stroked both hands down her back, feeling her slender waist and the gentle flare of her hips through the silk material of her dress. Obeying the hard pressure of his hands, Anabel strained closer. Clasping her hips, he pulled her lower body against him hard and crushed her mouth with his in desperation.

He wasn't sure what brought him to his senses, but all at once he knew he had to pull away from her. *Get control of yourself, Westby,* he cautioned himself, *or*

*you'll be making love to this woman right here on
her front porch.*

In a supreme moment of self-control he eased his
hold on her. Their lips clung an instant longer before
he drew away.

Her eyes caught the light and shone a soft silver
color as she looked up at him. For a moment her arms
remained locked around his neck, and then she shuddered, the spell shattered, and stepped back. He
barely heard her whispered good night as she slipped
into the house.

They made love for the first time two weeks later,
and it was a ravishment of the best kind. A mutual
ravishment of their senses and bodies that left them
stunned and forever altered.

At the age of twenty-eight Jud had fallen in love for
the first time. He fell hard and, as it turned out, so
deeply that he knew he'd never be quite the same
again. The next two months were the closest thing to
paradise he ever hoped to experience.

Then Tim died.

Jud had come to know the boy well since he started
seeing Anabel and had grown very fond of him. Tim
was bright and handsome and everything Anabel
said of him. A feeling of camaraderie and respect
developed between Jud and Tim.

Jud was as concerned as Anabel when Tim came to
the hospital with an acute appendicitis attack. Fortunately the boy was young and strong. The surgery
should have been a routine procedure followed by a
few days in the hospital and a speedy recuperation.

But the anesthetic machine or Jud himself had failed; after eight years he still wasn't sure which.

His life was shattered. While he was still trying to absorb what had happened, Anabel turned on him.

As Jud finished his martini, his head throbbed with the things she had said to him that night at the hospital.

You killed Tim! I'll never forgive you! Murderer!

Later that night, as he grieved for Tim, he told himself that Anabel had been hysterical; she hadn't known what she was saying. But she had meant it. When she returned to the hospital, she wouldn't speak to him, wouldn't even look at him. She tightened up every time he came into the same room with her. He couldn't take it. He left the hospital, his residency, everything.

Packing all he owned into his car, he started driving, not knowing where he was going, not caring. Somehow he ended up in a remote, forested section of Canada. He rented an isolated cabin and lived there for several months. Time and time again, he went over that night in the operating room, trying to discover whether he or the machine had been responsible for Tim's death, until he thought his head would crack. Eventually he realized that he was going to drive himself crazy if he didn't get on with his life.

The fascination anesthesiology had held for him was gone, and he couldn't generate any interest in resuming the practice. He went to Atlanta and was lucky enough to be accepted by a hospital there as a surgical resident. Slowly, painfully he had put his life back together again. Eventually he could sleep without dreaming of Tim, could go for hours without thinking of Anabel. He couldn't change what had happened eight years ago. He was human. He had made a mistake—a terrible mistake, but he wasn't the first doctor ever to have done so. And he had learned from what had happened that night in the operating room. He became a stickler for details. He had a reputation, among professional colleagues, for obsessive perfectionism. Not a few of them had been infuriated with him for intruding on what they considered their domain. With bitter irony Jud thought about the many times he'd been accused of being particularly hard on anesthesiologists.

His colleagues' outrage did not deter him. He continued to check everything in the operating room himself before beginning surgery. Those who worked with him learned to live with his perfectionism, or they didn't work with him long. In Atlanta, only a few close friends knew what was behind his checking and rechecking; everybody else thought he was simply compulsive.

Night came to Charleston, and the room darkened as Jud sat, holding his empty martini glass, remembering. During the past eight years he had tried to forget Anabel, tried to build relationships with other women. But sooner or later his memories of Anabel always intruded. That's why he had come back. He admitted it to himself at long last without excuse or rationalization. He had to know if there was the frailest remnant of what they once shared on which to build a new relationship. If not, he had to get her out of his system once and for all.

His jaw hardened as he remembered their meeting in the parking garage that afternoon. She had been so unrelentingly cold, hating him for coming back. God, she had changed. Yet in spite of everything his heart had quickened; his blood stirred at the sight of her.

Heaving a gut-deep sigh, he set the glass on the carpet and got slowly to his feet in the shadowy room. He had to shower and get ready for the reception where he would try to be cordial and smile and wonder how he could keep his face from cracking with strain. He didn't expect Anabel to be there. She had made it plain that she was going to avoid him like the plague. He sighed again and, picking his way through the darkness, headed for the bathroom.

He had made his decision, and there was no turning back now. He was in Charleston to stay, and he'd make the best of it. He'd be damned if he would let her ruin his life again.

As Mason came around to open the car door for her, Anabel smoothed the skirt of her crepe dress with both hands. It had taken her half an hour to make up her mind what to wear to the reception, and now she hoped she wouldn't be too conspicuous in the bias-cut emerald dress with its attached matching scarf draped around her shoulders. It wasn't the sort of thing she usually wore. Lucy had talked her into buying it to wear to the Tremaines' annual holiday party last Christmas. She hadn't worn it since. Her small clutch bag matched her high-heeled pumps, open at the toe and sides, in gleaming silver calf. She probably would have felt more comfortable in the black dress and shoes she had discarded in favor of the outfit she wore. But it didn't really matter. She didn't plan to stay long.

Nervously she tucked an imaginary strand of hair into her smooth chignon and smiled as Mason opened her door.

He cupped her elbow as she stepped out. "Did I tell you how beautiful you look tonight?"

She laughed, willing herself to relax. "Only three times." She fought a small tremor of panic, once more cataloging her reasons for calling Mason to say she would like to attend the reception after all. Attendance at hospital functions was expected of her, more so than of physicians in private practice. She was a salaried staff doctor, an employee of the hospital. Furthermore, she didn't want any rumors to start at the hospital concerning her attitude toward Jud. And she might as well get used to being in the same room with him. She would be serving on hospital committees with him; inevitably she would have to administer the anesthetic for some of his patients. The sooner she learned to function normally around him, the better.

She looked over at Mason as they crossed the brightly lighted hotel foyer. He was wearing a charcoal gray suit with a pale blue silk shirt and a brightly colored tie. "You look pretty spiffy yourself."

He winked roguishly. "I didn't think you noticed."

Before she could respond to his playful mood, they were swallowed by the crowd spilling out of the large wine-and-gold ballroom into the hotel foyer.

Taking her hand, Mason plowed through the crowd to the bar. "What'll you have?" he asked.

Anabel was busy surveying the crowd, seeing a lot of familiar faces, looking for Jud. She wanted to know where he was so she could steer clear. Then, without warning, her eyes collided with his across the large room. For a moment she was helplessly frozen, incapable of moving. He wore a dark suit and tie with a shirt of pristine white. His facial features had grown more sharply delineated, more arresting. The silver streaks at his temples glittered in the light from the huge chandeliers, in dramatic contrast with the dark hair and suit. Jud was the most striking man in the room; in her eyes he had always been the most striking in any group. The fact did not please her. The arrogance in the slight, acknowledging nod of his head angered her, releasing her from her frozen stance. But not before Mason noticed her preoccupation.

"Anabel?"

She glanced at him over her shoulder. "I'll have a spritzer."

Jud knew, through some sixth sense, the moment she arrived. While trying to keep up his end of a conversation with the chairman of the hospital board, he had scanned the room, looking for her. When he found her, he took in the fact that she had an escort. The man looked familiar, and a moment later, he was able to put a name with the face: Mason Kelsey, an assistant to the hospital administrator. What the hell was she doing with Kelsey?

"Don't you agree, Dr. Westby?"

Jud watched Anabel turn and say something to Kelsey, then realized that the chairman had asked him a question. Seeing Anabel with Mason Kelsey had caused him to lose the thread of the conversation. He had no idea what the chairman was talking about but chanced an agreement. "Certainly."

Accepting her drink from Mason, Anabel asked, "Don't you think it's stuffy in here?"

Mason eyed her with concern. "I hadn't noticed. You look pale. Are you sure you're feeling all right?"

She took a deep breath and sipped her wine. *Relax,* she ordered herself. *Stop acting like an idiot because you saw Jud. You knew he'd be here.* "I'm hungry. Let's find the hors d'oeuvre table."

Mason took her arm. "A woman after my own heart." There was relief in his voice, and it made her feel ashamed. He had been afraid she was ill and would have to go home. He seemed truly to enjoy her company, and that made her feel briefly guilty.

They finished their drinks and loaded small crystal plates with shrimp, tiny sausages, raw vegetable spears, dip, and crackers. They skirted the edges of the room, greeting acquaintances, finally stopping near the open doors that led to a balcony, enjoying the fresh air that wafted into the room.

Mason took her empty plate. "I'll get rid of these and get us another drink. You wait here."

She nodded and edged toward the balcony. Surprisingly there were only two people out there, a young, engaged couple who worked in the hospital laboratory. She smiled when she realized they'd been kissing. The young man turned around, saw Anabel, and blushed. "Hi, Dr. Dixon. How are you this evening?"

"Fine, and you?"

"Great." He was already urging his fiancée toward the door. "See you later," he called over his shoulder as they moved into the ballroom.

Anabel pulled her scarf around her arms, leaned on the heavy, iron railing, and looked out at the city lights. She'd fallen in love with Charleston at first sight, and it continued to beguile her. Part of its charm was knowing that it had survived great fires, earthquakes, Indian and pirate attacks, the Revolutionary War and the Civil War, while managing to remain a gracious city of church steeples, beautiful old walled gardens, and of houses with piazzas to catch the breeze. "Charleston is like all Southern belles," a native once told her, "all fragile and soft on the surface and tough as nails underneath."

Moonlight shone through the long cobwebs of moss draping the live oaks in the hotel garden. The flowers in the garden were mere shadows in the night, their fragrance light and entrancing, carried on the spring air.

With a soft sigh Anabel propped an elbow on the balcony railing and cupped her chin in her hand. Behind her she could hear the sounds of the reception's ebb and flow. Her scarf gave off the faint smell of cigarette smoke, absorbed while she was in the ballroom. She wrinkled her nose and took a long, refreshing breath of spring air.

Mason would bring their drinks, and they could finish them on the balcony, away from the noise and stuffiness of the reception. Then she would plead tiredness and ask him to take her home. He would want to come inside for a nightcap, but he wouldn't ask. Mason never asked. He seemed perfectly willing to give her all the space she wanted, which was the main reason she allowed him to escort her to these social gatherings. Mason Kelsey, she concluded, was a polite, considerate, intelligent man. And, above all, safe. She was in no danger of becoming emotionally involved with him. She smiled wryly, remembering the ripple of guilt she'd felt earlier. But perhaps Mason felt as safe with her as she did with him. Maybe he enjoyed her company simply because she was convenient. She hoped so. Lifting her eyes, she gazed up at the night sky. There were too many artificial lights around to be able to see the stars. When she got home, she would watch them glimmer from her bedroom window. She wished she was there already. What was taking Mason so long? A crowd at the bar, probably. Poor Mason.

"You're a good man, Mason," she murmured to herself.

"It's always nice to be appreciated."

With a quick gasp Anabel straightened and whirled around. Backlighted in the entrance to the ballroom, he was only a dark shadow, tall and lean. He moved toward her with the assured grace of an athlete. Jud's dark suit blended with the night, but his eyes reflected the soft garden lights. For an instant Anabel felt removed from the sophisticated city spreading all around her. She was isolated in some primitive setting, her vulnerability exposed. As Jud came toward her the garden lamps highlighted the chiseled planes of his face. He had never looked so fearfully dark and compelling to her.

"Where is Kelsey?" His voice was quiet, yet as unnerving as an unexpected shout over a loudspeaker.

Abruptly Anabel became aware that her hand was extended in the defensive pose she had struck as she whirled to face him. Carefully she lowered it to her side. It was only the unexpectedness of his seeking her out, she told herself, that made goose bumps rise all over her skin. "He's getting fresh drinks," she said tersely. "What are you doing out here? Don't you like being the center of attention?"

"Not particularly," he said, staring down at her. "I needed some air."

He was too close. She had to get away from him. "I suppose even fame and adulation can get tiring."

He merely looked at her, frowning a little and

spreading his feet as if to brace himself. "Are you involved with Kelsey?"

The sudden intensity in his tone sent a cold shiver up her spine. What gave him the right to ask her personal questions? She made a low, indignant sound. "That's none of your business, Jud." He shifted, and she caught a whispered scent of masculine cologne. *Maddening,* she thought as her stomach muscles contracted, *how clearly I remember that scent.* Why did the human brain persist in storing up memories that were best forgotten? She hated herself for feeling so abysmally trapped. What was wrong with her? She could simply walk away. She edged sideways, her back to the railing. "You must excuse me," she bit out with a rudeness calculated to rattle him. "I find I don't like the company out here."

He did not seem intimidated in the least by her insult. With ease and perfect timing his skilled surgeon's fingers closed around her upper arm as she swept past him. He swung her around to face him. "I don't want to fight with you, Anabel." He wasn't gripping hard enough to hurt her, but it was enough to keep her from escaping as she had intended.

Stunned by his closeness, the shockingly familiar feel of his hand on her skin, she was gripped by a numbing paralysis. She was aware suddenly of the sound of their heavy breathing. Her breasts brushed against his jacket, and his eyes, in the gentle light from the ballroom, were full of anger and pain. Her senses sprang quiveringly to life, too acutely aware of his touch and scent and the mute questions in his eyes.

Perhaps mistaking her stillness for a softening toward him, he hauled her to him and stopped her startled "no" with a demanding kiss. One bruising hand found the small of her back and held her against him. For a moment the kiss was all greedy taking on his part, and then she felt the abrupt gentling as it washed through him and he groaned against her mouth. For another moment she was too frightfully confused to do anything but let it go on. When his hand slid beneath her arm to mold around her breast, she stiffened. What bizarre mixture of hate and remembered love had made her submit even for a second? Wildly, blindly her fists thrashed against his chest. She pulled herself from him.

"How dare you." The words were low and filled with eight long years of outrage. She heard herself and was dismayed to realize that she sounded like the heroine of a second-rate melodrama.

Dragging air into his lungs, he raked both hands through his hair. He spoke in a tightly controlled voice. "Anabel, we have to forget the past. How long do you want me to suffer? I've paid for Tim's death many times over."

He could not have said anything more calculated to enrage her. As if anything could ever pay for Tim's death! "I hate you! I wish you had di—" She bit off the words savagely. In a flash she had seen herself as if from outside herself, and she was appalled at her complete loss of control. He wasn't worth losing her composure over.

Reflexively the muscle in his jaw tightened into a savage knot. "I know. You wish I had died instead of Tim. So did I, Anabel, for a long time."

Ruthlessly she squashed a feeling of sympathy at the abject pain in the words. He didn't deserve her sympathy. There was nothing more to be said between them. There hadn't been for eight years.

She had to find some inner strength to rid herself of all feeling for this man. Love had died with Tim. Hatred was debilitating. As for the stirrings she'd felt when he kissed her, and the flash of sympathy just now, she couldn't even begin to define their cause. All she knew was that she must school herself to feel nothing for Jud or she would end up being destroyed.

CHAPTER FOUR

Anabel met Mason returning from the bar, a drink in each hand. "I want to leave."

He stared at her. "Can't we have our drinks first?" He had seen her plunge into the ballroom crowd from the balcony. Her face was ashen, as though she'd received a shock.

She glanced about distractedly, further disconcerting Mason. Anabel's famous self-possession had deserted her. It was a jolt to see her upset and disoriented.

"Yes, all right." She took the glass of wine from his hand and swallowed half of it in one gulp. Another uncharacteristic action: Anabel usually nursed a glass of wine for an hour.

Looking over her right shoulder, Mason saw Judson Westby framed in the doorway to the balcony. He stood there for an instant, his hands shoved in his trousers pockets, frowning darkly and looking over the crowd with a glazed expression. Mason sensed that whatever the famous surgeon was seeing, it wasn't the ballroom; his mind was somewhere else.

Then abruptly, Westby bowed his head and struck out in the direction of the bar.

Mason put two and two together and couldn't believe what he came up with. He brushed the suspicion aside. "You look like you're going to faint. Are you?"

The color returned to her face as she fixed him with a contemplative look. He had the odd feeling that it was the first time she had really seen him since coming in from the balcony. A rosy flush invaded her cheeks, as if she were embarrassed; but perhaps it was just the wine. "Don't be so dramatic, Mason." She drained her glass and looked around for someplace to put it down. "I'm merely tired, and I want to leave. I should have followed my first impulse and stayed at home. Look, if you aren't ready to go, I can call a taxi."

"No." He took another swallow of Scotch. "I always leave with the woman I bring."

His intensely quizzical look grated on her already shivering nerves. She looked away as he took her arm to guide her through the crowd. They deposited their glasses on a table beside the door as they passed into the foyer. Neither of them spoke again until they drove away from the hotel. The only sound was the hum of the car engine and the distant sound of city traffic.

Mason's suspicion was back. He kept remembering the way Westby had looked, standing in the doorway. "What happened on the balcony, Anabel?"

61

The sudden question split the lulling silence harshly. She shot him a surprised look. "What?"

"I saw Westby leave the balcony right after you did. Did you two argue or something?"

She looked straight ahead, her hands clenched together in her lap. "I don't want to talk about it."

It wasn't the answer he wished to hear. He had hoped for a denial with enough feeling to convince him he was wrong. She sounded angry. Since he had known Anabel, he'd seen her angry only two times—both today, and both somehow linked to Judson Westby. He laughed uneasily. "Man, whatever he said, it must have really touched a nerve."

She suddenly rubbed both hands over her face. Alarmed, he wondered if she was crying. But when she looked up again, she was dry-eyed. "I should never have gone." She sounded so resigned.

"You knew him before, didn't you?"

It was so long before she replied that he thought she wasn't going to. She looked out the window, then stared at her hands. Finally she said, "He lived here when I was in medical school."

Assimilating this information, he took the turn leading to the Battery. Now that he thought about it, he wasn't really surprised. From her aversion to attending the reception, and the way she had looked when she'd come from the balcony tonight, it should have been obvious that she knew Westby. It was obvious, too, that they had been more than casual acquaintances. "He was a surgical resident?"

She shook her head. "Anesthesiology. Later he changed his specialty."

"Were you in love with him?" Mason asked, feeling that he had to know.

She was very still, thoughtful, as though the answer to that question was a difficult one. "It was a long time ago."

"And now?"

"Now I despise him."

Her voice trembled with emotion. Such intensity. Amazed, Mason reflected that Westby was the first man he'd ever known to arouse Anabel to any strong feeling. He glanced at her, saw the rigid set of her beautiful jaw, and realized that he actually envied Westby. Even loathing seemed somehow preferable to the bland absence of emotion that characterized Anabel's attitude toward Mason.

After a sleep-troubled night Anabel entered the doctor's lounge at eight-thirty the next morning. She was scheduled to give the anesthetic for two T-and-As back to back, beginning at nine-thirty. Having arrived at her office at eight, she'd dictated a couple of letters before going in search of coffee.

Several doctors already occupied the lounge, some in surgical scrubs, others in street clothes. Exchanging greetings, Anabel crossed the room. There was an open box of fresh doughnuts beside the coffee urn. She filled a Styrofoam cup and selected a doughnut.

She was stirring cream into her coffee, her back to the door, when she became aware—with alarming certainty—that Jud had entered the lounge. It wasn't the abrupt halt in several conversations or the obvious welcome with which he was received. It was an unnerving flash of intuition. Her body knew an instant before her mind did, and the pale hairs on the back of her arms stood on end.

Behind her somebody said Jud's name, confirming what she already knew. She stirred her coffee longer than was necessary, steeling herself to face him. She removed the plastic spoon from her cup and laid it on the table with exaggerated care.

Before she could turn around, a hand reached out to take a Styrofoam cup from the stack in front of her. She stared at the short, dark hairs on the backs of the long fingers and knew it was Jud's hand even before she lifted her eyes.

He bent slightly to fill his cup. He wore a light tan jacket and an open-collared, pale blue shirt tucked into the trim waistband of navy-blue trousers. His handsomely angled face had a smooth, just shaved, look; his dark eyes were clear and direct. She wondered if he had any idea how striking he was. As he straightened, full cup of coffee in hand, he seemed oblivious of everything except her.

"Are you all right?" His voice was low, private, but not at all apologetic. For an instant his eyes lowered to rest on her mouth, and she knew he was reminding her that she had responded to his kiss. Last night, before she had flown from him, her body had yielded meltingly in his embrace. She expected him to acknowledge her with coldness. Anabel was

64

braced for that. She was prepared to take some cutting remark about last night with aplomb.

She wasn't prepared for him to inquire about her in a solicitous tone or for his eyes to be so steady and deep with intimacy. For a long moment the conversations going on around them receded, and as clearly as if he had told her, she knew he wanted to unpin her hair and bury his hands in it, to crush her against him in a long, hotly possessive kiss. Her color rose and her thoughts scattered as the clean scent of his skin weakened her. His eyes held hers, and Anabel felt as though he saw through her clothing, saw all of her thoroughly.

Steadying a bit, she tried to make her voice sound more even. "I'm fine. Why wouldn't I be?"

"You left in such a state last night, I was worried." He said it calmly, though his look was fierce.

"Don't waste your time worrying about me, Jud." She spoke with such firmness that he lifted a brow.

"That's easy for you to say," he reflected, "but I can't help it." He wondered how he'd stayed away from her for eight years. Seeing her again had brought all the old feelings back with incredible strength.

In an unconscious gesture he lifted a hand, as though to touch her hair. She tossed her head back to make sure no contact was made. His hand fell to his side. "I've managed perfectly well without your concern for the past eight years."

He studied her. "Have you, Anabel?" His voice remained calm with just a hint of challenge.

"Yes," she snapped, her hard-bought composure threatening to crack. She turned away and sent an almost frantic gaze over the room, searching for a friendly face with an empty chair beside it. Several of the doctors were watching her interestedly, perhaps wondering what Jud and she were talking about with such concentration. For a horrifying instant faces swam before her eyes, unrecognizable.

Jud laid a hand on her shoulder. "Anabel, we have to talk."

She stiffened and made a quick, involuntary sound, as if she'd suffered an unexpected blow. "I told you," she said through wooden lips, "not to touch me." Her gaze fell on Bob Ohaleron, a white-haired obstetrician who occupied half of a short, green vinyl couch in the far corner of the lounge. Bob smiled at her, and stifling the flutter of fear Jud's touch had created, she shook off his hand and made a beeline for the couch.

"May I join you, Bob?"

"Please do."

Carefully averting her look from the place where Jud stood, she sank gratefully into the cool vinyl and the safety of Bob's fatherly presence. Anabel had always liked Bob, who planned to retire next year. In his late sixties, the obstetrician had treated her with friendliness and respect from the day she came on staff at the hospital. A widower, Bob often talked to her about his grandchildren, all of whom lived hundreds of miles from Charleston.

Bob watched Anabel settle into the seat beside him

and take a bite of her doughnut. He leaned toward her. "It's going to work out, Anabel."

Anabel glanced into his kindly blue eyes with an acerbic smile. Bob was the only other person present who knew the circumstances of Tim's death as well as about Anabel and Jud's relationship eight years previously. He knew because, soon after it happened, Anabel broke down in a moment of weakness and told him. The other doctors in the lounge had all joined the hospital staff during the intervening time. Even among those who had been there eight years before, few knew the details of what happened in the operating room the night Tim died. Operating room personnel didn't talk of what went on in surgery. It was a universal, unwritten law for which Anabel was, at the moment, very grateful. She couldn't have stood it if everybody in the hospital was watching her and remembering.

"Do you really think so?" she asked disbelievingly.

"Yes. Have you talked to him yet?"

"Briefly, last night. It was a mistake."

Hearing the desolation in her voice, Bob patted her hand fondly before sliding down in the couch and clasping his hands behind his head. He stretched his legs in front of him and gazed at the toe of his shoe. "Did I ever tell you about my first patient?"

Grateful for the change of subject, Anabel said with a chuckle, "No, but something tells me I'm going to hear about it now."

"That was, let's see . . ." Bob continued to squint at his shoe. "Almost forty years ago. I had a general practice in a little country town in Kansas. The nearest hospital was thirty miles away, and it only had twenty beds. The first day I opened my office, a young woman came to me, pregnant with her first child. She was a robust farm girl, big-boned and rosy-cheeked. I didn't foresee any difficulties."

"What you OB people call a baby machine," Anabel said dryly.

"Exactly. The pregnancy and delivery should have been a breeze."

The sad note in his voice touched Anabel. "It didn't turn out that way?"

"Everything went along well until a couple of weeks before the birth. Then she started coming to the office or phoning me almost every day, complaining of a pain here and a pain there. Twice she went to the hospital, convinced she was in labor when she wasn't. I put it down to her youth and inexperience, because every time I checked her, the baby had a good, strong heartbeat and was in the proper position. Everything seemed completely normal. She and her husband were a couple of kids living out in the sticks, fifty miles from the hospital and twenty miles from the nearest town. I don't think there was a neighbor within a mile. I thought they were just scared she'd have the baby before she could get to the hospital."

"Seems a natural assumption," Anabel murmured, finishing her doughnut and licking her fingers daintily.

"Finally she went into labor, and her husband

brought her to the hospital. I delivered a healthy, eight-pound boy. The next morning, when I made rounds, she was still complaining of pain in her stomach. I'll never forget her lying there, trying to be brave, smiling at me through her tears. She apologized for being such a bother, said she didn't know she would keep hurting after the delivery, but she thought it was getting better. The nurse on duty took me aside and assured me the girl was just suffering from postpartem depression. I shouldn't have delayed any longer, but I wanted to believe the nurse. So I waited twenty-four hours. The girl was still complaining of severe pain, and I scheduled exploratory surgery. When I cut her open, I discovered that she'd had good reason to complain. Adhesions caused by old appendectomy scars had caused bowel blockage. The girl died on the table."

He still hasn't forgiven himself completely, Anabel thought, even after forty years. "The pregnancy disguised her other problem," she said.

"If I'd taken her complaints seriously earlier, I might have saved her. She'd been in trouble for at least two weeks, but I kept telling myself, It's her first baby—she didn't expect any discomfort—and there's usually discomfort in the last few weeks of pregnancy. I tried to make excuses for myself, Anabel, but I had to go and tell a young father that the mother of his baby was dead. It was years before I got over it. For a long time I drank heavily, almost drank myself to death. Eventually, with the help of my wife, I pulled myself out of my self-flagellation, closed my office, and started an OB-Gyn residency. I've never been back to that little town to this day."

Anabel put a comforting hand on his arm. "Bob, most young doctors would have reacted as you did. You can't still blame yourself."

He turned his head, looked at her gravely. "I don't carry around the guilt anymore. I had to accept the fact that I'm human, and even in medicine, there is sometimes human error. We have to forgive human frailties, our own and other people's. We have to learn to accept the things we can't change, Anabel."

She knew why he had told her the story, even though it still hurt him to remember it. His intentions were totally unselfish and well-meaning, but she wasn't sure she could equate Jud with Bob. She shook her head sadly. "I know what you're trying to do, Bob, and I appreciate it. But I have to work this out for myself."

As Bob talked she had become acutely aware of Jud watching them from across the room. Now, suddenly, it seemed too close in the lounge. She finished her coffee and went to check the board where the surgery schedule for the coming week was posted.

Bob's story lingered in her mind as she hurried along the wide hall. But Tim's case was not the same as the young woman's, she told herself. Jud had been negligent; she could never excuse that.

She found the schedule and ran a fingernail down the line of names beneath "Anesthesiologist." The first listing of her name was in the Monday noon slot, and tracking the line back, she read the surgeon's name: J. Westby. Her heart dropped. She had hoped she wouldn't be scheduled to work with Jud so soon.

She looked over her shoulder and saw Jud coming out of the lounge, hurrying, his jacket flying open. Anabel's senses were so acutely honed that in a single instant she took in the dark lock of hair falling over his forehead, the silver-streaked sideburns feathering back over his ears to frame his face, the lithe movement of his long, athletic legs.

"Anabel," he called, his deep voice filling the hallway.

Two surgical nurses walked by; they said something to Anabel and glanced in fascination at Jud as he approached. Anabel smiled as if in response to what they'd said, but she hadn't taken it in. Her mind was blank, and she felt her strength dissolving as she gazed into Jud's face. Blinking, she came to herself and, turning, walked swiftly away from him.

Several times during surgery, her mind drifted to Monday, when she would have to share an operating room with Jud. *I'll get somebody to substitute for me,* she told herself. *I'll go to Mason and refuse to work with Jud.* But Mason didn't have the final say in such matters. He would have to go to the administrator. What reason could he give for such a surprising request? Indeed, what reason could she give a colleague when she asked him to substitute for her in surgery Monday? The assumption would be that she was intimidated by Jud's reputation.

By the time she left surgery at noon, she had gotten herself in hand. Finding a substitute for Monday

71

would only postpone the inevitable. And going to Mason with her problem would be unprofessional. Above all, Anabel prided herself on maintaining a professional attitude. The only professional thing to do was to give the anesthetic for Jud Monday.

She didn't see Jud again before she left the hospital Friday afternoon. She usually enjoyed her weekends, cleaning house, stocking up on groceries, and planning menus for the coming week, visiting Lucy and Bill. But she didn't find this particular weekend enjoyable; it provided too much time to think about Monday. On Saturday afternoon she called Lucy and suggested that they go shopping for spring dresses. Bill was working, and Lucy welcomed the opportunity to get out of the house.

They headed straight for their favorite shop in the mall a few blocks from the Tremaines' town house. As they rifled through a rack of pastel print silk dresses, Lucy said, "So, how was the reception?"

Anabel replied absently, "Like most such affairs. Too crowded. Tedious. You stand around, trying to balance a plate in one hand and a drink in the other while engaging in social chitchat with people you see every day. I didn't stay long."

"Did you talk to Jud?"

"Briefly." Anabel lifted a daffodil-splashed dress from the rack. She had a weakness for yellow. "Look, Lucy, isn't this lovely?"

Lucy didn't particularly like yellow herself, but the bright dress was such a change from Anabel's usual plain, tailored wardrobe that she agreed wholeheartedly. "Ummm, yes. With your height you can wear big prints. Why don't you try it on?"

In the dressing room Lucy sat in a straight-backed chair and watched Anabel extract her long, shapely legs from her jeans. "How did it go? With Jud, I mean."

Anabel pulled the dress over her head. "We only exchanged a few words," she said evasively, her voice muffled by the silk material. Her head appeared, and she fastened the fabric belt around her slender waist. She turned in front of the mirror to look over her shoulder and survey the back of the dress. "What do you think?"

"I think it's a little sick to hold a grudge for eight years."

Anabel's head snapped around. "Stop it, Lucy. I was talking about the dress."

Lucy met her eyes steadily. "The dress looks wonderful on you, Anabel. You don't need me to tell you that."

"Oh, Lucy." Passing a hand over the smooth line of her drawn-back hair, Anabel turned to stare at herself in the mirror. "I'm sorry. I didn't mean to snap at you. I don't want to hurt the best friend I have in the world."

"What is it you *do* want?"

"To be left alone. To be able to do my work without interference. To go home at night and feel I've spent a satisfying day practicing my profession."

"And now Jud has entered the picture to distract and disturb you."

73

"I'm afraid I can't work with him without letting my feelings take over," Anabel said quietly. "I'm scheduled for one of his surgeries Monday, and I'm not sure I can carry it off with as much competence as usual. My feelings are so mixed. I'm afraid he'll find fault with my performance, and I'm actually mad at myself for worrying over what he might think. Isn't that stupid?"

"No. You've got a lot of suppressed emotions when it comes to Jud, and they're going to haunt you until you work them out, come to terms with them."

With a bitter smile Anabel turned back to the mirror. "I think I'll buy this dress. The price is outrageous, but what the heck. I can afford it."

As they were leaving the shop, Anabel said, "A new dress calls for new shoes. Isn't that always the way?" She halted, realizing that Lucy was no longer beside her. "Lucy?" She turned to see her friend leaning against the shop's showcase, her hand spread against the glass as though she needed the support. Anabel ran to her side. Lucy's face was pale, blue-tinged. "Lucy, what's wrong?"

"I felt dizzy," Lucy said faintly. "Don't get excited. I'm all right now."

"Of course, you are," Anabel said, slipping an arm around Lucy's waist. "You're so all right, you're going to drop right here in the mall if you don't rest for a while. Come on."

Lucy didn't argue, and Anabel found a place for the older woman to sit down. After a few minutes, when Lucy's color had returned a little, Anabel helped her through the shoppers and into the car. Lucy put her head back against the seat and closed her eyes. She was still much too pale. Anabel kept glancing at her worriedly as she drove to the town house. Inside, she tucked Lucy into bed and examined her as well as she could without her bag. When she started to leave the room, Lucy called her back.

"Where are you going?"

"To call Nathan Osborne."

Lucy sat up in bed. "No! I do not want to see my cardiologist."

She was so agitated that Anabel hesitated, then returned to the bed and urged Lucy to lie back down. "I think he should check you, Lucy. He should know what happened at the mall."

Lucy shook her head on the pillow, her eyes wide in her white face. "I'm better now. I don't want you to call him. And you have to promise not to tell Bill what happened."

Anabel sat down on the side of the bed, baffled by Lucy's attitude. "I don't understand. You're a nurse, Lucy. You know what happened today could be serious."

"No," said Lucy adamantly. "I will not go into the hospital."

"You don't even know that Osborne would suggest that."

"Yes, I do."

Anabel stared into her friend's fiercely stubborn

75

eyes. "He's told you you should have surgery, hasn't he?"

Lucy looked at her stonily for a moment, then nodded. "He's talking about valve replacement, Anabel. I simply won't agree. Bill doesn't know that Osborne's recommended open-heart surgery, and I don't want him to find out. If you tell him, I'll never forgive you."

Anabel was flabbergasted. Practical, sensible Lucy had decided to ignore her serious condition, as though it might go away on its own. "Lucy Tremaine, what's wrong with you? You know the risk you're taking by doing nothing."

"Promise you won't tell Bill," Lucy insisted.

Lucy's color was slowly improving. Anabel sighed. "I promise, for the time being."

"Thank you. As for my doing nothing, you're wrong."

"Oh?"

"I found a wonderful book."

"A book," Anabel repeated blankly.

"It was written by a Swedish doctor. He claims to have cured heart conditions with vitamins and herbs and a special diet."

Anabel looked at the ceiling, exasperated. "I can't believe I'm hearing this. If you didn't have any medical knowledge, I might understand. But, Lucy, you know better. Vitamins and special diets are fine, but they won't grow a new heart valve, I don't care what some Swedish doctor says."

Lucy closed her eyes, as though the conversation

76

had worn her out. "I'm going to give the regimen a fair chance," she said wearily. "Surgery is an absolute last resort, and I won't have it unless I reach the point where I'd rather die than live the way I am."

"It's not like you to be so fatalistic."

"My mind's made up. Don't waste your breath trying to change it. You can go home now. I'm going to take a nap."

Anabel stood, looking down at the outlines of Lucy's slight body beneath the sheet. Suddenly she looked very fragile. "Fat chance. I'm staying here until Bill gets home."

"Suit yourself," Lucy murmured, "just so you don't tell him. . . ." Her voice trailed off, and Anabel tiptoed out of the room, leaving the door open so she could check on Lucy periodically without waking her.

Obviously Lucy had convinced herself that she would not survive surgery. It was so unlike her usual optimistic outlook; Anabel couldn't understand it.

CHAPTER FIVE

By Monday, Anabel had prepared herself to work alongside Jud with impersonal efficiency. But when she arrived in the OR early to find Jud already there, checking out the anesthetic equipment, she lost her professional cool.

"What are you doing?" she demanded. She was so furious, she was shaking.

Ignoring her hostile tone, he finished his methodical inspection. Straightening up, he surveyed her with perfect calm. They both wore hospital scrubs. The sturdy green cotton material molded itself to his chest and broad shoulders as though the suit had been made especially for him; curling black hairs were visible in the dip of the V-neck.

"Just making sure everything's okay."

Wiping her palms on the seat of her pants, she managed to get a tenuous hold on her outrage. "For your information, Dr. Westby, I don't need your help in checking out the anesthetic equipment. I'm perfectly capable of doing it myself."

Jud gave her a long, steady look. "It never hurts to have a second opinion."

Anger flared in her eyes, anger she barely managed to suppress. She heard female voices; two of the surgical nurses had entered the suite and were just beyond the OR doors. "I won't stand for your put-downs, Jud," she said as calmly as possible. "Stay out of my way."

"Or what?" he murmured, his voice deceptively mild.

"Or I'll lodge a complaint with administration," she returned evenly. "I'm the anesthesiologist, you're the surgeon. Is that understood?"

"Yeah." He had a raging urge to catch her close, crush her mouth with his, force the angry rigidity of her body to yield. Why was he letting her make him so mad? She was far from the first doctor to complain that he'd overstepped his territory. He should be used to it by now.

She glared at him as he stared back with the insolent cocksureness that so enraged her. If he ever checked up on her again, she would take enormous satisfaction in lodging a formal complaint. Turning on her heel, she strode toward the scrub room. Two nurses, their eyes as big as Frisbees, stood just inside the OR, the door open behind them. They'd probably heard every word. They murmured tentative hellos and moved hastily aside as she stalked past them. In the scrub room the two assisting surgeons looked at her questioningly; clearly they'd heard the exchange too. She nodded curtly, picked up a brush, and started scrubbing. By tomorrow the whole hospital would know about the flare-up between Doctors Westby and Dixon; such clashes didn't qualify for hush-hush status in the unwritten laws of medical ethics. Fuming, Anabel hoped Jud would give her half a chance, outside of surgery, to unload her temper on him. She couldn't remember when she had been so angry; she was wound up for a fight.

Scrubbing her hands and arms until they stung, she forced herself to push her personal feelings down for the time being while she became strictly an anesthesiologist.

Once the patient was wheeled into the OR, Anabel concentrated only on him. She performed her duties adroitly, uttering not a single unnecessary word during the long and difficult surgery. She didn't have to watch Jud to know he was in his element. In one swift glance she saw his intense concentration, the iron steadiness of his skilled hands, the beads of perspiration glistening on his face that were regularly wiped away by one of the nurses. Several of the hospital's surgeons had gathered on the other side of the room's huge observation window to watch the procedure. They're all awed by Jud, Anabel reflected with distaste; but even she had to admit that his performance was letter-perfect.

By the time the surgery was finished and the patient was wheeled into recovery, her scrubs were wet with perspiration. The tension between her and Jud had added to the usual strain of the life-and-death situation. She was totally wrung out, doubtful that her legs would carry her to her car. She decided to relax in the lounge for a bit before dressing and going home and was relieved to find the room unoccupied.

Anabel was sitting on the vinyl couch when Jud walked through the door. In an instant she was on her feet. He glanced at her as he walked to the coffee urn. Like her, he had hardly a dry stitch on him. Damp strands of dark hair stuck to his forehead, and fatigue slackened the chiseled lines of his face.

"Dammit," he muttered, "there aren't any clean cups." He turned around, his eyes measuring her. "Still bent out of shape, aren't you?"

The insolent question was all it took to bring her temper flaring to the surface again. "The whole surgical team heard us."

"I'd say so, yes. I didn't think it bothered you."

"When a surgeon acts as if I don't know my job, that's what bothers me!"

"You're taking this too personally," he said quietly.

Heart hammering in her throat, she tossed back, "It is personal, Jud. You only checked the equipment because I was the anesthesiologist, and you made sure I'd catch you at it. It was pure spite."

She took grim pleasure in the flash of anger in his eyes. "That's ridiculous. I always check everything in my operating room."

"*Your* operating room! My God, you've become a prima donna."

A surgical resident entered the lounge. Jud sent him a disinterested glance before retorting, "I treated you no differently than every other anesthesiologist I work with."

By then Anabel was too fired up to worry about being overheard. "Oh, really?" she inquired with icy sarcasm. "Well, don't expect this anesthesiologist to take it."

A muscle in his rigid jaw clenched spastically. "I will continue to do as I've always done," he said, measuring the words out with deadly precision, "no matter who the anesthesiologist is. You, of all people, should understand my extreme caution."

"Oh, I understand, Jud," she said, flaring, "but in my case it isn't necessary. I haven't killed anybody yet!"

His hand snaked out to grab her arm. She caught a quick glimpse of the resident's gaping face as she twisted viciously away from Jud and stormed from the lounge.

She didn't look back to see if he was following her as she slammed into the women's dressing room and, with shaking hands, stripped off the wet scrubs. She stood for a full five minutes in the shower, letting the hot water pound her. She had stopped shaking by the time she stepped out. She dressed and went to her car without seeing Jud. When she noticed his Mercedes parked near her Buick, she concluded he had gone to check his patient after cleaning up. The dedicated doctor—first, last, and always, she told herself with a mixture of acrimony and grudging respect.

Too keyed up to be hungry, she passed over the chicken-noodle casserole waiting in her refrigerator in favor of a small serving of cottage cheese. She was about to spoon the cottage cheese from the carton when her door bell began to ring insistently.

Her shoulders sagged. If that was Lucy wanting to hear about her afternoon in surgery with Jud, she simply wasn't up to it. Hurrying to the door, she yelled, "Get off the bell. I'm coming!"

She opened the door and saw who it was. And before she could do anything, Jud pushed his way into the foyer.

She rushed past him to bar the door into the living room. Banking the flood of mingled fear and excitement he had caused within her, she nearly spat at him, "Get out of my house."

He brushed past her as though she were as insubstantial as a spiderweb. He stood in the center of her living room, feet spread, thighs stretched taut. He raked a restless glance over her beloved plants and chairs and books, as though he might be thinking of breaking something. "We haven't finished talking," he said, his voice deep and rough with suppressed wrath.

"I've finished." She faced him with flashing silver eyes, her voice shrill. "I want you out of here. Now!"

She might as well have ordered a wall to move. His look was hard, implacable, and she was gripped with bitter helplessness. He wasn't going to leave until he was ready—not her house or her life. He was a force to be reckoned with now, personally and professionally, as undeniably as the earth turning on its axis. This man, whom she had loved and hated, with his iron will, virility, and passion, was not about to get out of her life!

She jerked her eyes away from the mesmerizing fire in his. "Go away. Leave me alone."

"What happened today must never happen again."

"Oh, indeed, Doctor," she challenged as her chin came up. "Are you making the rules for everybody at the hospital now?"

He ignored her attempt at ridicule. "The next time you have a bone to pick with me, don't do it in the lounge or the OR or anywhere else where we can be overheard. I will not provide a sideshow for my colleagues."

"I'll pick bones with you wherever and whenever I choose. I don't *care* whether you like it or not! Can't you get that through your head? You come back to Charleston, march into the hospital as though you own the place, order people around with your . . ." Tears constricted her throat. She covered her face with her hands. "With your damn reputation and arrogance!"

He came toward her, his eyebrows drawn together darkly, alarm making itself felt beneath his anger. "Anabel . . ."

Lifting her head, she retreated inch by inch until her back was against a solid wall.

"I didn't come here to get into another argument with you. I don't want to hurt you."

White-faced, she shook her head. "I don't believe you. Your mere presence in Charleston hurts me."

He towered above her, his jaw set, his lips an un-compromising line. "It doesn't have to—if you'll only let go of the past."

Pushed beyond the point of caution, she flared, "Just pretend Tim never existed? Forget that you murdered him?"

Overcome by unbearable frustration, blinded by the injustice of her accusation, he was hardly aware of what he did. Snatching her in an inflexible grip, he hauled her like a rag doll against him. The softness of her body was exactly what the rough hardness of his clamored for. Her hair came unpinned and fell in a silvery tangle around her head. The smell of soap and her light cologne seduced and enflamed him. She gazed up at him, frightened but defiant.

He had no control over what he did. He crushed her mouth with his and felt the ache of desire. He hadn't come there to prevail by superior strength. He had meant to clear the air with reasonable discussion. He'd had no idea that remembered cravings could be so easily resurrected. For a moment the need for her was all-consuming.

Faintly the recognition of what he was doing hammered in his fevered brain. She was as rigid as a stick in his arms, but underneath the rigidity was a trembling. My God, he never meant to frighten her. He wanted her soft and clinging, her eyes glazed with desire for him, the way she had been with him so long ago. He wanted that more than anything. But he didn't know how to make it happen.

"Anabel," he said, moaning, lifting his mouth from

85

hers, letting the grip of his arms around her relax. "I'm sorry." Desperate for her forgiveness, he let his lips roam her white face, soothing, caressing. "I lost my head. I didn't know what I was doing. I came here, thinking we could start over like two strangers, but there's too much between us for that. We have to admit our feelings. We'll never have any peace otherwise."

The contrite words and whispered kisses touched her in places angry male dominance could never reach. A thrill shot through her, and she knew it would be the easiest thing she'd ever done to turn her head and capture his questing mouth with hers, to shut out the past that screamed for recognition and turn to liquid pliancy in his arms. Tears trickled down her face.

"Don't cry, Anabel," he muttered against her lips, his tongue tasting the salt of her tears. "Please don't cry."

With a miserable moan of self-loathing, she felt his hard arousal as he lifted her to him. Oh, God, how could it be so easy? "I hate you for this," she whispered even as she felt herself melting inside.

"I know."

His humble acknowledgment of her feelings gave her a trickle of courage. Between them they had touched bedrock truth. There was no need for pretense now. "If you keep on, I don't think I'll be able to say no," she admitted. "But I want you to stop. Please."

The taste of her flesh and her tears ravaged his

senses, and he knew he could go on feasting on the delights of her body. He could fill his hands with her breasts and her hips and slide with her into the dark abyss of sensation. But it wouldn't be fair. Afterward there would be yet another wedge of distrust between them. He wanted her desperately but not without her wholehearted cooperation.

Slowly he lifted his head. Her eyes were heavy with passion that pushed at the restraints she was trying desperately to keep in place, and in the gray depths there was pleading. He closed his eyes, still holding her gently, and warred with the primitive need for her that lay in him like an iron weight.

The faint sound of her despairing whimper struck him like a blow. He looked down at her, overcome by a vast need to protect her. "There's never been another woman in my life who could touch you," he said soberly. "I don't think there ever will be."

Anabel didn't trust herself to reply. She was paralyzed by the clash of her mind's horror and her body's betrayal.

Jud released her and stepped back. "Forgive me."

She stood amid her cherished belongings, enclosed by the walls of her beloved home, which had, until now, provided all the security she needed. But there was no protection anywhere when Jud could storm her fortresses simply by touching her. She turned her head aside, blond hair swirling like silk around her shoulders. Forgive him? That wasn't the point. Could she forgive herself?

Slowly she felt strength returning to her limbs, and

she stepped away from the support of the wall at her back and, with great effort, looked into his eyes. "I—I owe you an apology too. For what I said to you in the lounge in front of the resident. You're right. We should settle our differences in private."

Her tone was defeated, her face pale. Such vulnerability wrenched at Jud's heart. He wished he knew what to say or do to restore her defenses. In that moment he hated himself.

"Anabel—"

"Please go."

His shoulders slumped as he turned away from her. Subdued, he left the house, the door clicking softly behind him.

The whole world seemed still, as though it were aware of the enormity of what had happened in Anabel's living room. She stood as evening extended its shadowy fingers across the carpet, blurring the corners of the room. Her thoughts were full of self-rebuke; despair and guilt washed over her. Then, with a small cry, she hugged herself fiercely, as though she could crush that aching part of her that throbbed with such pain after lying insensate for eight years. She had turned her back on that vulnerable core of herself, had wanted and believed it dead. She had built a meticulous and ordered life on that belief.

Now her simple, precise existence lay around her in shambles, and she didn't know if she could put it back together again. How could the man who had destroyed her life once demolish it again with a kiss?

What was wrong with her, that she could allow it to happen?

More than ever before, she knew the life she had built for herself as Dr. Anabel Dixon was a lonely one. But she had been satisfied these past eight years to fill her days with work, while remaining unaware of the depths of her loneliness. Her hand fluttered to her breast, and she touched the softness that had been pressed forcefully against Jud's hard chest. For one insane moment she wished Jud had entered her life for the first time a week ago, that she could blot out the past completely and forever.

"No, no, no," she whispered. "Don't be a fool."

The ring of her telephone brought the outside world crashing in on her. The sound seemed an alien intrusion in the quiet house, shaking her from her despairing thoughts with a jolt. Without turning on any lights, she walked with carefully measured steps to the kitchen and lifted the receiver from its hook.

She tried to speak but had to clear her throat before she could say, "Hello."

"Anabel? You sound funny. Are you sick?"

Anabel collected her thoughts. "No, I'm not sick, Lucy. And stop stealing my lines. How are you feeling?"

"Wonderful. I took a long walk this afternoon, and it felt great."

After what happened Saturday at the mall, Anabel no longer accepted her friend's assurances without reservation. Nor was she completely at ease with her decision to help Lucy keep Bill in the dark about the attack. "When are you going to see Nathan Osborne again?"

"Soon," Lucy said vaguely, "if I don't decide to change doctors."

"Just so you see somebody good," Anabel persisted.

"I'm thinking of making an appointment with Jud."

"That's not a bad idea." Perhaps if a second doctor told Lucy she must have surgery, she'd believe it. Regardless of what Anabel thought of Jud personally, she knew he was the best heart man around.

"Speaking of Jud," said Lucy transparently, "how did it go in surgery today?"

There was no point in beating around the bush, Anabel thought. Lucy always knew when she was being evasive. "We had words."

"In the OR?" Lucy sounded shocked.

Anabel sighed. "He was checking out my equipment when I arrived. We were the only ones in the room at the time, and I told him I resented it. But, after surgery, in the lounge, it got worse. I completely lost my cool and said something I should never have said. To make things worse, there was a resident there, and he heard everything. Jud was furious."

"Well. What was the outcome? What did he do?"

"Followed me home."

Lucy made a sympathetic clucking sound. "What on earth did you say to him?"

"I said he didn't need to check my equipment because I hadn't killed anybody yet."

"Good Lord, Anabel! That's the worst thing I ever heard. How could you?"

Lucy was taking Jud's side! It made Anabel feel more defensive than ever. "It just slipped out, Lucy. He made me so mad, I didn't know what I was saying. Then, when he followed me home, I called him a murderer. He was in a pure rage. Oh, Lucy, it was awful."

"It's a wonder he didn't hit you."

"No, he didn't hit me." She thought perhaps she could have dealt with that better than his kiss. "I apologized."

"Well, I should hope so. I've never known you to lose your head like that. But I guess it's not too surprising, considering the way you feel about Jud."

"I may blame him for Tim's death, but I'm going to have to learn to keep it to myself."

Lucy made a sound of impatience. "That's not what I'm talking about."

"I don't understand."

"You're still in love with him, Anabel."

Fear exploded in Anabel. "That's preposterous!" she sputtered. It wasn't true! "I have to hang up now, Lucy. I'll talk to you later." She broke the connection before Lucy had time to respond.

Restlessly she moved to the wall switch and turned on the kitchen light. The carton of cottage cheese was still on the counter. She spooned some into a bowl and sat at the kitchen table.

Still in love with Jud? Impossible. Why would Lucy say that? The cottage cheese tasted like paste; she ate it automatically, her mind whirling. Physical desire was one thing; love, quite another. Yet why was it that she had never felt a stirring of desire for any man except Jud? Her body had been as good as dead since Jud went out of her life. But at the reception those long-dormant feelings had stirred as soon as he had kissed her. Today they had become uncontrollable.

Dear God, Lucy couldn't be right. Of course, she had strong feelings about Jud. She had hated him for eight years! That's why he could arouse her emotions as no other man could. That didn't mean those emotions were love, did it?

Anabel groaned and, pushing the cottage cheese aside, laid her head on her folded arms atop the table. She closed her eyes, and suddenly she remembered what Bob Ohaleron had said to her that day in the lounge: "We have to forgive human frailties, our own and other people's. We have to learn to accept the things we can't change, Anabel."

Bob was a wise man. Perhaps it was time, she admitted, to let go of the anger and guilt over Tim's death. The past could not be changed. If-onlys were futile mental exercises, and she'd indulged in them long enough. She, better than most people, knew that life was too full of death and pain to live indefinitely with self-inflicted added hurt. Maybe if she could forgive Jud, the disturbing power he seemed to have over her would go away.

Even now a part of her resisted. Wouldn't forgiving Jud be a betrayal of Tim's memory?

She buried her face in the darkness created by the circle of her arms. How would it feel to be free of resentment after so long? As though the world's weight had been lifted from her shoulders, she admitted. Jud's intentions had been only to help, to heal. Because of that, he had been able to come to terms with Tim's death. Shouldn't she? Where should the blame be placed finally—on Jud, on the machine, on fate? Perhaps in the abyss beyond sight and consciousness where all unresolved dilemmas were eventually discarded so that people could bring a semblance of reason and order to the chaos of their lives.

A semblance. Was human existence, then, ultimately only chaos? Was there really no reason, no order—no love that transcended simple animal needs? No, she could never believe that. Her heart had swelled too many times as she watched critically ill patients given new life on the operating table. Using her skills, exhausting herself for sick people gave her life a purpose. As for love, she had seen it in the faces of too many worried wives and husbands, parents and children, to believe it was an illusion.

Love was all around her, no less real because she didn't share in it. She was the exception, not the rule. She was on the outside looking in, and she had never been more aware of it than at that moment. Finally she fell asleep there at the kitchen table. It was the middle of the night when she awoke and made her way through her empty house to her lonely bed.

CHAPTER SIX

Within a few weeks Anabel knew that Jud had told the truth when he said he hadn't treated her any differently from any other anesthesiologist. One of the senior anesthesiologists had been incensed when he'd entered the OR and found Jud methodically checking out everything in the room, including the oxygen outlets and the anesthetic equipment. An indignant complaint to the hospital administrator was countered by a rambling dissertation on the necessity for doctors and support personnel to give themselves time to become accustomed to Dr. Westby's "way of doing things." In time, promised the administrator, everybody would come to understand and appreciate Dr. Westby's "unique approach" to his work. Though placatingly stated, the message was clear: Jud's colleagues would adjust to his methods, not vice-versa.

Knowing she had not been singled out helped to dissolve much of Anabel's anger. Ironically she even found herself defending Jud one Friday afternoon when Gretchen repeated a juicy rumor that was floating around the hospital.

"I heard Dr. Sullivan refused to assist Dr. Westby in surgery today," Gretchen said. "Seems Westby raked him over the coals yesterday in front of the whole OR team for not being alert enough."

Anabel was well aware of the divorced Sullivan's reputation as a swinger, and she knew that he had appeared at the hospital hung over on too many mornings. In the past she had felt the surgeons with whom Sullivan worked were too lenient with him. Rallying around to protect a colleague at a difficult time in his life was one thing, but keeping silent when a doctor was in no shape to be treating patients was another.

"If that's true," Anabel said dryly, "I imagine Sullivan was merely anticipating Jud's refusal to have him assist a second time. Can't say I blame Jud, either. It's been over a year since Sullivan's wife left. The old 'divorce shock' excuse won't wash anymore. Sullivan's life-style is detrimental to his performance as a surgeon." Anabel wasn't telling tales out of school. Everybody in the hospital knew about Sullivan's drinking and carousing. Charleston was too small a city for a physician to keep an irregular private life private for very long.

Gretchen lounged easily in the doorway to Anabel's office. It was four-thirty, and the suite was quiet, Anabel's associates having left for the day. "Boy, you're the last person I expected to hear defending Westby," Gretchen said, and grinned at Anabel's flustered look.

Anabel removed her reading glasses and cleared her throat. "I hope I can still give credit where it's due, Gretch."

Gretchen folded her arms and propped a hip against the door frame. She was wearing a red float dress with embroidered flowers on the hem ruffle, red patent sandals, and huge, dangling silver earrings. "Mighty generous of you, Doc, I must say. After that dust-up you had with Westby."

It was the first time Gretchen had mentioned the OR incident, now almost three weeks in the past, but Anabel wasn't surprised that the tale had already made the rounds. "We got that straightened out." She made a neat stack of the medical files on her desk. "Jud's a perfectionist in the operating room, not the easiest trait to deal with in a colleague but preferable to carelessness."

"Did you really accuse him of killing somebody?"

Anabel smoothed her hair before looking up at Gretchen. "Does that sound like me?" Oh, clever, she told herself.

"Not really. I can't see you losing your cool to that extent, but I do get the feeling that you're upset about something lately."

Anabel shifted her shoulders uncomfortably. She wished Gretchen weren't so direct, but the secretary didn't know any other way to be. "As it happens, I've had a lot on my mind lately. And getting used to working with a new surgeon, particularly one of Jud Westby's caliber, hasn't helped the situation."

"Um-hmmm." Gretchen fingered the silver loop of an earring, pursing her lips in thought. "I'm an outstanding listener, Anabel, if you ever need a sympathetic ear." At Anabel's uncertain look she added hastily, "I'm not trying to be nosy."

"No?" The mild rebuke brought an unabashed grin to Gretchen's face.

"Well, maybe a little. Hey, I couldn't help but notice that your jitters and Westby's tenure at the hospital started at the same time."

"Jitters! I haven't been jittery, Gretch. Have I?"

At Anabel's startled stare Gretchen laughed. "Let's just say that everybody in the office has been tiptoeing around you the past couple of weeks. Dr. Adler asked me yesterday if you ever suffered from premenstrual syndrome."

"He didn't!"

"Yes, he did." Gretchen watched closely as Anabel rose from her chair and went to stare out of the window. "I told him I didn't think your menstrual cycle had anything to do with it."

"How do you like that?" Crossing her arms, Anabel rubbed her hands absently over the long sleeves of her blouse. "A man can be as temperamental as he likes, and nobody asks if he's had his testosterone level checked recently. But let a woman have a bad day, and it has to be hormones."

"Are you sure it *isn't* hormones?"

With an uneasy laugh Anabel turned away from the window. "What are you talking about?"

Gretchen met her eyes steadily. "Jud Westby. You said you knew him years ago, and my woman's intuition tells me you were more than friends."

Anabel tried to pass it off lightly. "Woman's intuition? Really, Gretchen."

"Okay, call it my vast experience in dealing with the opposite sex," Gretchen returned with a mischievous smile. "I've been in love at least a dozen times. I know the signs." She cocked her head, and the silver bangles hanging from her ears sparkled with reflections of the bright ceiling lights. "I knew someday somebody would come along who'd knock you off your pins."

"You've got it all wrong," Anabel said, her quiet voice without rancor. "I've just been working out a few problems. Things are getting back to normal now. I'm sorry if I've made it unpleasant for you around the office."

"No sweat." Gretchen straightened as if to leave, then paused to wink and say, "It's no crime to fall in love, you know, Doc. And if you are . . . well, I just want to say that Jud Westby has my stamp of approval."

With a helpless laugh Anabel made a shooing gesture with both hands. "Go home, Gretch."

"I'm going, I'm going."

In the outer office Gretchen tied up a few remaining Friday strings, then called a cheery "Have a good weekend" as she left. A heavy silence fell, and Anabel returned to her desk, not to work but to sit and think.

Things *were* getting back to normal, she told herself, in spite of what Gretch said. She had worked with Jud several times in the past three weeks. His looking over the anesthetic equipment no longer angered her. It didn't thrill her, of course, but now that she knew it wasn't intended as a personal insult, she could tolerate it.

The first few times had been tense, to be sure. But gradually she was getting used to being with him in surgery and could relax more. In fact, she had discovered that working with Jud could be exhilarating in a way that nobody outside of medicine could fully understand.

That special high that came when the OR team, against all odds, pulled somebody back from the threshold of death could be found nowhere else. It had happened with one of Jud's patients earlier that week, and Anabel knew she wouldn't soon forget the throat-clogging elation she'd shared with the other members of the team.

The patient was a sixteen-year-old girl named Carrie, who suffered from a congenital heart condition. Having been a semi-invalid all her life, Carrie was no stranger to hospitals. Until recently the state of the art in heart surgery had not progressed to the point where the risk, in Carrie's case, was worth taking. During the past year Jud and a few other cardiovascular surgeons around the country had perfected a new technique that could be used in cases like Carrie's; the chances of surviving to live a normal life were statistically about sixty to forty, against. But Jud said the statistics were inaccurate since the procedure had been improved since the first few cases.

As was her custom, Anabel went to see Carrie in her hospital room the day before the surgery to describe the type of anesthetic she would be getting and how it would affect her, and to answer any questions the patient might have. People were less apprehensive about being anesthetized if they knew what to expect. It was Anabel's first meeting with the girl. Knowing of the seriousness of Carrie's condition, Anabel didn't look forward to the interview and put it off until late afternoon.

She expected to find a terrified teenager, probably angry about the cards fate had dealt her, and almost certainly spoiled by parents who lived with the constant fear that each day of life might be their daughter's last. But she was wrong on all counts. She had rarely seen such courage and serenity, even in patients much older than Carrie. The girl was beautiful with that tissue-fragile, blue-veined skin sometimes seen in the chronically ill. Carrie's long auburn hair was bound in a single braid that hung down the back of her lacy pink nightgown. Her brown eyes lit up when Anabel entered the room; clearly she was lonely and wanted somebody to talk to.

"Hi, Carrie," Anabel said. "I'm Dr. Dixon, your anesthesiologist."

"Oh, good. You're going to tell me about the stuff you'll use to knock me out. Dr. Westby already explained what he's going to do to my heart. That I can grasp. I mean, it's pretty mechanical, don't you think? But I've never been able to figure out how anesthetics work. Maybe you can explain it to me."

"I'll do my best." Anabel pulled a chair over near the bed and sat down. The girl sounded so cheerful, Anabel couldn't help but wonder if she fully understood the seriousness of what was going to happen the next day.

Carrie listened intently as Anabel gave her a simplified version of how certain substances such as nitrous oxide and thiopental sodium, when injected into the bloodstream and carried to the brain, caused unconsciousness and loss of feeling in the entire body.

When Anabel had finished, Carrie lay back on her pillow, her eyes wide. "That's so mysterious."

"It is," Anabel agreed, "and a great blessing for people who have to undergo surgery."

"Oh, yes, I'm really thankful I don't have to get my chest cut open while I'm awake." A flicker of unease, the first Anabel had detected, passed across the girl's face. "Dr. Westby will know when I'm completely out, won't he? I mean, I wouldn't want him to start too soon."

Anabel smoothed strands of auburn hair away from the girl's face. "We have ways of knowing when it's time. I guarantee he won't start too soon."

Carrie sighed. "Good," she said, then flashed Anabel a smile. "I won't worry then. This is my decision, you know. My parents and Dr. Westby told me what the odds are, and they let me make the choice. You look sad, Dr. Dixon. Please don't be. I believe I'll make it through the operation. I want so much to be able to do what everybody else can do. After this is over, I'm actually going to take tennis lessons. Maybe I'll even get a horse."

Anabel blinked rapidly to stave off tears. It was a miracle how Carrie could be so optimistic and confident after the life she'd led. She was emotionally mature for her age, not spoiled at all. There was something about her that reminded Anabel of Tim. If she were allowed to live a normal life, she would draw other youngsters to her like a magnet. Steadying, Anabel said, "Carrie, you've got a wonderful future ahead of you."

"I think so," said Carrie seriously.

Anabel stayed to chat with the girl for half an hour. When she rose to leave, Carrie asked, "Dr. Dixon, do you believe in God?"

"Yes."

"Then would you say a prayer for me?" A sweet smile curved Carrie's lips. "I know you and Dr. Westby are great, but I'd like to have God on my side, too."

Impulsively Anabel bent to press a kiss on the pale forehead. "You got it. With a team like that in your corner, you can't miss, kid." She left Carrie chuckling.

The operation was long and tedious, with none of the light talk and joking that often went on during surgery. Everybody was poignantly aware of the desperate battle the beautiful teenager's body was fighting on the table. It humbled and subdued them.

As the operation progressed, their hope built and by the end, when they knew, barring unforeseen complications, that they'd beaten the odds, they were in a state of elation. It was only the second case in which Anabel had been involved when several members of the surgical team cried unabashedly and hugged each other as the patient was taken from the OR. Anabel cried and hugged, too, and before she realized who it was, Jud was holding her. Euphoric, she hugged him back. As they left the suite, Jud's arm slung over her shoulders, he asked her to have lunch with him to celebrate. In her elated state she agreed.

They went to a restaurant a block from the hospital because Jud didn't want to be far from Carrie for the next twenty-four hours. Conversation was easier than Anabel thought it would be. During the half-hour they spent together before Jud rushed back to the hospital, they talked of Carrie's operation and the hospital. Once or twice Anabel caught Jud studying her carefully, but thankfully he didn't refer to what had happened at her house three weeks earlier.

When they parted in front of the restaurant, she was buoyed by relief and gratitude. *It's going to be all right,* she concluded. *We can share a professional relationship without letting personal feelings come into it.*

It really was working out, she told herself again as she left the office that Friday afternoon. She wasn't all tied in knots as she'd been ever since Jud's return;

she was actually looking forward to a free weekend. As she passed from the hospital into the brilliance of a Charleston spring, she decided she would play tourist that weekend, something she hadn't done in ages. She'd browse through the market in the historic district, visit some of the old churches, and have lunch in one of the touristy cafés. She was humming as she headed for the parking garage.

The last person she expected to run into in the historic district Sunday afternoon was Jud. It was three o'clock when she came out of the old Huguenot Church on Church Street and, arms swinging, followed the cobbled street to the open-air market. She wore comfortable walking shoes with her new daffodil-splashed dress, which she'd donned on a whim, because it was such a beautiful day and she felt light-hearted for the first time in weeks. The shoes and dress were an incongruous match, but she didn't care. Having nowhere else to wear the dress, she'd decided it was as appropriate as anything else for a trek through Old Charleston. In a hurry to leave the house earlier, she hadn't taken the time to pin up her hair, instead tying it at the nape of her neck with a ribbon.

In the market she browsed over a table of large handwoven baskets for several minutes, debating whether to buy one and have to lug it back to the car. Deciding against buying, she turned, stepped away from the table, and collided with Jud.

Surprised, they both broke into laughter. Reaching

out, Jud steadied her, saying, "I wasn't sure that was you. Your hair's different."

For a split second, before she turned, he wondered if he was dreaming. The slim figure in the gaily colored dress, the blond hair tumbling down her back, had reminded him so much of the Anabel of eight years ago that he'd halted to stare as he ambled through the market. *It's your fertile imagination,* he'd told himself. *She's a stranger, probably as ugly as a post.* Then she'd turned around.

He wore khaki trousers and a white polo shirt. "What are you doing here?" she asked.

"Getting reacquainted with Charleston." He raised a brow and stepped aside as an obese woman waddled her way to the basket table. "Excuse me, ma'am." The woman was reaching for a basket and didn't even look back. He shook his head, amusement lurking in the corners of his eyes as he looked down at Anabel. "What's your excuse?"

She smiled. "The same, I guess. I haven't been down here in almost two years. I get so involved with work, I forget there's a whole other world out there."

"I know what you mean."

She stood looking into his chiseled face and was seized by a sense of strangeness. He seemed different in his casual attire, his dark hair wind-ruffled. Like the old Jud. The last thought slipped into her mind before she knew it was coming. It was accompanied by a sudden self-consciousness, and she clamped down on it. "Well, I'd better be on my way."

"Are you meeting someone?"

106

She hesitated. "Not exactly," she responded with a trace of defensiveness in her voice.

His relaxed expression tightened into a scowl that unexpectedly struck her as funny. "What does that mean?"

She chuckled, deciding it was futile to try to be cagey. "It means, no, I'm not meeting anyone. But it's a long walk back to my car, and I haven't seen half the merchandise in here yet." She began edging her way through the crowd toward a booth where scented candles were being sold.

Jud followed. "Know what I'd like to do?"

She glanced over her shoulder, surprised to find him still with her. Stopping, she turned to face him. "What?"

"Take a tour boat out to Fort Sumter. We did that on our second date. Remember?"

It had been a balmy May afternoon, much like today. She'd been thrilled when Jud asked her for a second date a few days after their first dinner together, knowing she was already half in love with him. How could she ever forget? But she hadn't expected him to remember.

"Jud, I really can't—"

"Okay." He grazed his knuckles over her cheek. "No reminiscences. Just come with me and we'll avoid memory lane."

He has a day off, and he's bored, she thought, vaguely amused. But then, he knew so few people in Charleston; with his work schedule he had little time to meet people other than professional associates. He was at loose ends and lonely, and she was unaccountably touched.

"Promise?"

He brightened, pleased to hear anything but the flat no he'd expected. "Sure. Whatever you say."

All at once she could think of no good reason not to go with him. He seemed so different away from the hospital, and she was different, too, if only outwardly. Standing in the midst of the jostling crowd of shoppers, she felt none of the tension that was often between them at the hospital. It would be a help, professionally, if they could establish an easier relationship. And the market could wait for another day. "Okay."

He fought to keep a silly grin off his face, and he had to remind himself again that this was not the Anabel of eight years ago. "We can take my car to the marina. It's parked about a block from here. Come on."

Taking her hand, he cleared a path for her in the crowd. When they reached the street and could walk side by side, he continued to hold her hand, and she didn't pull away, not wanting to make an issue of a triviality.

But it seemed a good idea to Anabel to find some common impersonal ground. "How's Carrie today?"

"Better than we had any reason to expect. I saw her just before I came out here. She even made a joke about all the hardware she's attached to. She's one tough little scrapper."

Anabel's throat tightened unexpectedly. Carrie

had really gotten to her. "I'm so glad. She's such a special girl. She told me she's going to take tennis lessons and get a horse."

Jud laughed. "I wouldn't bet against her."

They reached the marina only minutes before a tour boat left the dock. Jud bought their tickets, and they ran down the pier to board. There were no seats below, so they sat on deck and watched the gulls swooping and circling behind the boat, snatching popcorn tossed to them by some of the passengers. The wind grabbed Anabel's hair and whipped it across her face.

Jud caught her hand as she tried to retie the ribbon. "Let it go." She looked so carefree with her hair blowing about her face, so sweet and vulnerable that he longed to bury his hands in her hair. The mere thought of it sent flashes of pleasure searing through him.

She shrugged and, tossing her hair back, poked the ribbon into the purse slung over her shoulder. "It's a hopeless tangle, anyway. I'll do something with it later."

Jud had put his arm along the back of their seat, and his fingers toyed with her hair. "You remember Lucy Tremaine? Used to be a nurse at the hospital."

She shot him a startled look. "Remember her? She's my best friend."

"I didn't know that." He continued to caress her hair. "Well, you're aware of her heart condition then. I examined her the other day. Didn't she mention it?"

"No." Not surprisingly, Anabel thought. Lucy was being very secretive about her condition these days. She wondered if Lucy had even told Bill she'd seen Jud. "Her former doctor told her she should have value-replacement surgery."

"I know. I got her records from Osborne, and I concur with his diagnosis."

"You told Lucy that?"

"Of course."

"What was her reaction?"

"She promised to think about it."

Anabel sighed. Jud's fingers had insinuated themselves beneath her hair and lay warmly on the back of her neck. "I hope she will. She's been following the advice in a book written by some quack, trying to cure herself with a herb-and-vitamin regimen. I tried to tell her that wasn't going to solve her problem."

His fingers massaged gently. "You need to relax," he told her. Giving in to the gentle movement of his fingers, she closed her eyes and didn't see Jud's slow smile. "Heart patients have to have time to accept the idea of surgery."

"Ummmm," Anabel agreed absently. With the sharp scent of his skin in her nostrils, and his fingers massaging the tense muscles in her neck, she felt weak, as though she could sit there like that forever. "Maybe you should have Carrie talk sense to Lucy."

His fingers relaxed and rested on her shoulder. She let her head fall back against his arm. "Give her time. Some people need more than others to adjust. In the end it's the patient's life and his decision."

They sat in silence for a time, until Jud asked quietly, "What's going on between you and Mason Kelsey?"

The question, seemingly from out of nowhere, made Anabel's muscles tense up again. "Mason and I are friends."

He was silent, pondering her reply, until they docked and followed the other passengers off the boat.

Once they were inside the walls of the fort, they eschewed the trained guide's spiel and, still subdued, drifted away from their group toward the museum. Anabel took a sudden detour to examine a Civil War cannon in one of the gun rooms facing the parade ground. Jud reversed his direction to follow her.

She was behind the cannon in the shadowed gun room, running her hand over it. "Can you imagine shooting one of these things?"

He walked directly to her and did what he'd been dying to do for the past half-hour. He pulled her to him, claimed her mouth with a long, possessive kiss that barely hid a trace of desperation.

In a dim corner of her brain Anabel realized that she had been expecting this. Perhaps she had even gone into the dark and private gun room to make it happen. She didn't know, and now was not the time to try to figure it out. All she could do was lean against him as molten waves of desire shattered through her. She would have to be stone not to respond to the desperation she felt in him. It would take a stronger woman than she not to be caught up in his need. The weakness that had assailed her on the boat was back in double force as she grew faint with the taste of his mouth on her tongue, the feel of his thick, wind-blown hair between her fingers.

Like a man coming from watery depths for air, Jud lifted his head and looked into her heavy-lidded eyes. Anabel felt mesmerized by the stormy depths of his eyes. "I want you," he said quietly.

"Oh, Jud . . ."

They heard voices approaching. He stepped away from her, but only slightly, and combed his fingers through her hair, feeling its silken smoothness. "You want me, too."

Anabel's equilibrium was returning. "Don't you think you're being a bit presumptuous?"

Smiling, Jud continued to smooth his hand over her hair. "But honest. Come on, admit it." A middle-aged couple peered into the room, hesitated, and moved on.

"No." Anabel was pleased to hear the firmness in her voice, and she stepped out of his arms.

Jud cocked his head. "No, you don't want me? Or no, you won't admit it?"

She tossed her tangled hair back and, although it was difficult, met his steady gaze. "I don't want to talk about it."

"Just like that? When I've spent three long weeks dreaming about making love to you?" he said with a hint of a smile.

She saw that he was telling the simple truth, but she didn't want to know that he'd been dreaming about her. She didn't think she could cope with it. "I'm sorry. Maybe it was a mistake for us to come out here. I thought it would be good if we learned to relax with one another. We have to work together, and I wanted to make it easier for us."

"It's easy for me already. Maybe you're tense because you're afraid to admit how you really feel about me."

Her eyes flashed at his sardonic tone. "I'm tense because you persist in saying things like that."

"That's just my point," he returned, studying her. "It wouldn't bother you if there wasn't some truth in what I say."

"I don't intend to become your lover, Jud."

"So you have thought about it."

"It's pretty hard not to," she snapped, "the way you come on to me every chance you get."

"I haven't noticed you fighting me off."

The truth hurt, made her color rise and her temper flare. "My mistake. After this I'll make my feelings clearer." She swept past him, but he caught her arm and turned her around.

"Don't lie to me, Anabel. Don't lie to yourself."

"Let me go."

"Anabel . . ." Why had he allowed her to turn this into another battle of wills? All he wanted to do was pull her into his arms and comfort her, but he knew she wouldn't accept it. "I'm sorry. I keep saying things I have to apologize for, but I'll try to do better. Give me another chance?" He wasn't going to get through her defenses with a few kisses. He'd need patience to overcome the barrier of Tim's death between them. They would have to talk about it eventually, but this wasn't the time or place.

Anabel stared at him for a long moment, then let out a deep breath. "All right."

"Would you like to go to the museum now?"

His smile was disarmingly sincere. Before she realized it, she was smiling back. "Yes." They started across the parade ground, and she didn't pull away when he linked his fingers through hers.

CHAPTER SEVEN

It wasn't finished between them.

The truth was like a messy, unwelcome visitor in Anabel's orderly house. Upon her return from Fort Sumter, the clashing emotions that filled her when she was with Jud drained away, leaving only guilt. She stood before Tim's photograph and wept, convinced she had betrayed him that afternoon. Possessed by the beauty of the day and the thrill of Jud's presence, she had ambled over the grounds of the fort, talking and laughing, hand in hand with the man responsible for her brother's death. Confusion reigned in the precise and logical brain of Dr. Anabel Dixon, and she was tortured by remembered voices:

I've paid for Tim's death many times over.

We have to learn to accept the things we can't change.

You promised, Anabel!

There was no escape. The sanctuary of her home, the last bastion of serenity and certainty, had been invaded. The chaos was in her head; she carried it with her wherever she went.

She still had strong feelings for Jud! No matter how horrified she was by the knowledge, how much she hated herself for her weakness, it remained true. In the heavy silence of her bedroom, while she stared into the photograph of Tim's smiling face, she finally admitted to herself that eight years had not been time enough to blot out what they had been to each other.

Eventually her tears stopped, and she turned away from Tim's picture. Denial wouldn't work anymore. She must do what any reasonable person did when confronted with a bitter truth—deal with it as intelligently as possible.

She considered the possibility that Lucy was right: She might still be in love with Jud. Her intelligence told her that no emotion, even love, could live forever without nourishment. Love needed to feed on thoughts of its object. The solution was to put Jud out of her mind.

Brilliant, she chided herself. How do you manage that when you see him five days a week at the hospital?

Okay, she had to see him at work, but she didn't have to let him intrude on her own time. Angrily she stripped off her flowered silk dress—the betraying garment that had helped beguile her into forgetting the past that afternoon—and hung it in the back of her closet. She grabbed a brush and attacked her tangled hair, wincing when the bristles caught in a stubborn snarl. When the blond tresses fell smooth and straight around her shoulders, she pulled them back tightly into a neat braid, which she coiled at the nape of her neck. Then she put on a tailored beige blouse and matching slacks.

A prim and composed Dr. Dixon gazed back at her from the dresser mirror. Except for a lingering wistfulness in the gray eyes, she had succeeded in banishing the blithe and foolish Anabel who had made her unexpected appearance that afternoon. Now she would find something to do that evening, something to keep her mind off Jud.

A dinner guest, perhaps? Fortunately she had purchased filets and fresh mushrooms at the supermarket yesterday. She'd call Mason and ask him to come over.

It was the first time Anabel had invited Mason to dinner. His voice on the phone sounded surprised and obviously pleased. Anabel brushed aside a worry that she might be giving Mason the kind of encouragement she had no intention of following up. *We're friends,* she told herself. A friend doesn't read hidden meanings into a dinner invitation.

But from the moment Mason arrived, dressed in an expensive gray silk suit that made her simple slacks outfit seem positively grungy by comparison, she knew she'd been wrong. Mason handed her a bottle of French wine and a dozen red roses.

She was so embarrassed, she stuttered. "You—you sh-shouldn't have."

"I wanted to." His quick glance swept over her, and his ruddy complexion became even ruddier. "I guess I should have asked you what to wear."

117

Anabel recovered herself. "Oh, it's all right. Take off your coat and get comfortable while I take care of these."

She put the wine on ice and the roses in a vase, which she set on the dining room table. Dinner was not too uncomfortable, since they talked about the hospital. After dinner they went into the living room with glasses of wine. Anabel sank down on the Victorian love seat and, after a moment's hesitation, Mason sat beside her.

Their conversation became stilted, with long silences between sentences. Mason finished his wine, and Anabel drained her own glass, thinking he would go home now. She turned to set her empty glass beside his on a table, and when she turned back around, his arms engulfed her. Without any warning he was kissing her.

His mouth was wet and seeking, and Anabel felt nothing but acute embarrassment. In some remote part of her mind, she thought, there must be a dozen women who would respond eagerly to such ardor from Mason. All Anabel could do was wonder frantically why she hadn't seen it coming and how she could gracefully extricate herself. But there was no graceful way.

She wrenched her mouth from his and got to her feet in one motion. "Mason, stop."

He looked up at her, blinking, thrown totally off-balance. She should never have encouraged him by inviting him to dinner. He fumbled with his tie, which was askew, and, red-faced, mumbled, "I'm sorry, Anabel. I thought . . ."

Shame washed over her. She'd used Mason to keep her mind off Jud. No wonder the poor man was confused. "It's not your fault. It's mine. I invited you over for dinner and conversation because I didn't want to be alone this evening. I obviously gave you the wrong impression, and I apologize."

He got awkwardly to his feet and reached for his jacket. "I'm glad you asked me," he said, stuffing his arms into the sleeves.

She laughed nervously. "Still?"

He looked at her gravely. "Still, Anabel. I like being with you, even on your terms." He flushed. "I got a little carried away . . . I won't do it again. I don't want to do anything to make you stop seeing me."

"Oh, Mason," she said, sighing. "You're too good to me. Of course, I want to see you. We're friends." But no more intimate dinners, she added silently. No more mixed signals. No more taking advantage of Mason's good nature to ease your heartache over Jud.

Later, as she lay in bed, memories of the afternoon flooded over her again. "Get out of my life, Jud Westby," she muttered in the darkness.

When she entered the office Monday morning, Gretchen had a huge grin on her face.

"What's up?" Anabel asked.

"Something for you on your desk."

Anabel swept into her office, dropping her attaché case on a chair. A long white florist's box resided on

119

her bare desk. Gretchen had followed her. "It was just delivered."

"Who's it from?"

"Hey, I might be insulted if I was the touchy sort. You don't think I read the card, do you?"

Anabel threw Gretchen an apologetic smile. "Of course not." She unbuttoned her linen jacket and draped it over the back of a chair, all the while eyeing the gold seal on the top of the box bearing the name of a local florist. She remembered the roses Mason had brought last night and doubted that he would send more flowers as another apology, would he? Oh, dear, she hoped not. There wasn't even anything to apologize for. That embarrassing moment in her living room had been entirely her own fault.

But who else might send her flowers? With an odd reluctance she untied the ribbon and lifted the lid.

Masses of daffodils filled the box. Moisture-dotted, brilliant yellow, they looked almost too bright and lovely to be real. With a gasp of surprise Anabel gathered them into her arms. Closing her eyes, she buried her face in their faint, springtime fragrance. Velvet-smooth petals brushed her nose and cheeks. She held them away from her to admire them. Never had she seen anything so beautiful.

"I'll get a vase. Or several. I don't think one will be enough," Gretchen said, and left the room.

A small, white envelope lay in the bottom of the box. Laying the flowers carefully on her desk, she pulled the card from the envelope: "You should always wear daffodils."

Anabel dropped the card into her skirt pocket. She would read it again and again during the day. Gretchen returned with three vases, and they arranged the yellow flowers on a corner of the desk, on top of the two-drawer file cabinet and on the low bookshelf next to the window.

"Who sent them?" Gretchen asked.

"The card wasn't signed."

Gretchen's green eyes sparkled. "Ah ha! An anonymous admirer. Very interesting."

A thrilling shiver passed through Anabel. It could only be Jud. She could see him so clearly, his hair tousled by the wind, reaching for her hand, telling her to leave her hair free. She could feel his hand graze her cheek, the simple gesture as intimate as his kiss. Later she would seek him out in the lounge and thank him. The rush of heat she felt told her she was eagerly anticipating the moment. To hide the fact that she was reacting like an adolescent girl with a serious case of puppy love, she said briskly, "Enough of this. The world of medicine awaits. Would you call Dr. Isom and see if they've set a time for that committee meeting?"

It was late afternoon before she finally got to the lounge. She had timed it to arrive after Jud's last surgery for the day, hoping to find him alone, having a cup of coffee as he usually did when he left surgery. He was there, but so were the two surgeons who had assisted him. She greeted them and helped herself to coffee. As she stirred cream into her cup, Jud de-

121

tached himself from the other men and came to her side.

She smiled at him. "Thank you for the daffodils," she said quietly. "They're beautiful."

"I've been imagining you in your office surrounded by them all day." He studied her soberly. She seemed genuinely pleased about the flowers. But he wasn't sure it meant anything beyond the fact that she liked daffodils. He'd driven by her house Sunday evening. Mason Kelsey's car had been parked outside. She might have been just as pleased if Kelsey had sent the flowers. How long had Kelsey been at her place Sunday? Had he spent the night? Jud himself spent a restless night, thinking about Anabel and Kelsey together and trying to hold on to what Anabel had said at Fort Sumter: she and Kelsey were merely friends.

She flushed prettily. "That's flattering, but I don't believe it. You've been in surgery all day." *This is the way to handle it*, she thought. *Don't take his flirtatious remarks too seriously. Be cool.* "I have to get back to the office," she said brightly. "Thanks again, Jud."

He watched her leave, bewildered by her casual manner. Had yesterday afternoon meant nothing to her? He mumbled an absentminded good-bye when the other doctors left the lounge and stood at the window, pondering the change in Anabel between yesterday and today. He had thought he'd made some progress with her yesterday, but today she seemed to have withdrawn from him again.

In actuality Anabel was a mass of quivering nerves

122

when she left the lounge. It will get easier, she told herself stoutly. It has to. After cleaning off her desk, she left the hospital and ran into Mason just outside.

He brightened at the sight of her. "Anabel, I was just thinking about you."

She took his arm companionably, and they walked toward the parking garage. "You were?"

"Yeah, I wanted to apologize again. For last night."

He sounded so repentant that she had to laugh. Impulsively she leaned toward him and kissed his cheek. "No apologies needed, Mason. Forget it. I have."

He smiled, thinking, *That's just the trouble. I can't forget how you felt in my arms.*

In the lounge Jud was still standing at the window. He saw Anabel and Kelsey leaving, arm in arm, and he saw Anabel lean over to kiss Kelsey. He experienced a stab of jealousy stronger than any he'd ever known. It angered him. *She doesn't belong to you anymore,* he lectured himself. *She can kiss anybody she chooses.* But every time he closed his eyes, he could see her with Kelsey.

The memory bedeviled Jud all evening. He spent another restless night, arriving at the hospital Tuesday morning, cranky and gaunt-faced. Mason Kelsey was eating breakfast alone at a table in the VIP lunchroom when Jud arrived. Fate, he told himself dourly. He went straight to Kelsey's table. "May I join you?"

"Sure. Glad to have you, Dr. Westby."

Jud unloaded his tray and sat down. Kelsey was

123

about Anabel's age, he decided, and he supposed that boyish grin was attractive to women. After two sleepless nights Jud was too weary to be very subtle. He wanted information, and he didn't feel like trying to be sly about it.

"I understand you had dinner at Anabel's place Sunday evening."

Kelsey looked startled. "Uh, yes, as a matter of fact, I did. She's a fine cook."

"A special lady," Jud muttered.

"Well, I guess anyone can see that. She's intelligent, a good doctor. She's beautiful—"

"And she can cook," Jud finished, almost growling.

Kelsey stared at him, baffled. "Yes. Is there some problem, Dr. Westby?"

Jud glared back at Kelsey for a moment. He emptied a tiny container of cream into his coffee and stirred sloppily. Hot coffee splashed on his hand, and he jerked back, dropping the spoon. "Hell." He grabbed a paper napkin and wiped his hand and the pool of coffee that had sloshed on the table. "I'll lay it on the line, Kelsey. I want to know how you feel about Anabel."

Jud saw from Kelsey's expression that he'd made him angry. *No wonder, you bumbling fool*, he told himself. Kelsey looked him straight in the eye and said candidly, "I care for her a great deal. She's the most wonderful woman I've ever known."

The man's got taste, Jud grumbled silently, *I'll give him that.*

124

Kelsey stacked his dishes back on his tray. "I have an early meeting. Good day, Doctor."

He's in love with her, Jud thought, watching Kelsey go. Maybe she loves him, too. Why else would she have spent Sunday evening with Kelsey instead of Jud? He'd made it clear he had no plans, but she'd ignored his hints. Damn, what a way to start the day.

The following Monday morning Anabel entered her office to find the daffodils shriveled and drooping. She loved the way they'd brightened her workplace, and she dumped them into the trash can with regret. Without the daffodils to remind her, she had trouble believing that the afternoon with Jud at Fort Sumter had really happened. He'd been so reserved and distant with her since then. It was bewildering. Perhaps he regretted what had happened at the fort and had decided that the only relationship they could have was a professional one. Exactly what she concluded last week, so why did the change in him hurt so much?

She was glad she wasn't scheduled in surgery that day. She stayed close to her office, working until past five, and didn't see Jud at all. Her phone was ringing as she let herself into the house. Dropping her attaché case and purse on a chair, she ran to answer.

"Anabel . . ." The female voice was fragile, breathless, hardly more than a whisper.

"Lucy, is that you?"

For a moment there was only labored breathing on

the other end of the line. Then, "I fainted. . . . I think I was out a long time . . . I don't know."

Anabel had to strain to hear. "Is Bill there?" she asked sharply.

"At work. . . . I don't know what to do, Anabel. I'm scared."

"Lie down and take some oxygen. I'll be there as fast as I can."

Anabel hung up and ran from the house, grabbing her purse as she went. She found Lucy with the mask from a portable oxygen container over her mouth, laboring for breath and slightly disoriented. Anabel didn't hesitate; she phoned for an ambulance. Hanging up, she then got Jud's home phone number from information and dialed.

He answered after three rings, sounding tired but alert in the way that doctors trained themselves to be, even when they were exhausted.

"Jud, it's Anabel."

"So it is." He sounded surprised. "Hello, Anabel."

For a moment the sound of his voice made her feel weak. Then she gave herself an inward shake and spoke briskly. "I'm at Lucy Tremaine's house. She passed out, and she's still a little confused. She's having trouble breathing, even with oxygen. I've called an ambulance."

"I'll meet you at the hospital." The lulling tiredness was gone from Jud's voice; he was all competence now.

"Thank you, Jud. See you in a little while."

She phoned the office of the tour company for

126

whom Bill worked, but there was no answer. Bill could be somewhere between the marina and Fort Sumter, or he could be on his way home. She scribbled a note to him on the pad beside the phone, then went to check on Lucy.

Lucy watched her approach, her green eyes wide and frightened above the mask. Anabel sat on the bed beside her and put a comforting hand on her arm. "Just relax and try to breathe deeply. The ambulance is on the way."

Lucy's eyes glazed over for a moment. "I'm so sorry, Anabel. I've caused so much trouble."

Lucy's fingers twitched on the mask; she was still quite agitated. Anabel said soothingly, "Because you called me when you needed help? What nonsense is this? I love you, Lucy. I'm thankful I was at home when you called."

With a sudden movement Lucy clutched Anabel's hand. Anabel squeezed gently, trying to impart reassurance and comfort through the contact. "I've let it go on so long," Lucy said, wheezing. "I was just so afraid. Can you ever forgive me, Anabel?"

Dismayed, Anabel watched her friend struggle for breath. *Is she asking me to forgive her for putting off the surgery so long?* Anabel wondered. *She's disoriented and doesn't know what she's saying.* "Shh, Lucy. There's nothing to forgive. We're going to take care of you now. Just relax."

"No!" Lucy insisted, her fingers clutching tighter, "You have to forgive me."

Anabel would have said anything to pacify Lucy,

who probably wouldn't remember any of this later. "I forgive you. Now, be quiet. Please."

Lucy released Anabel's hand and, closing her eyes, seemed to sink deeper into the bed. She breathed quickly, shallowly, and it seemed like an hour instead of ten minutes before Anabel heard the siren.

She followed the ambulance in her car. She waited in the hall, pacing back and forth, while Jud examined Lucy. After a while he came out, looking grave. "She's drifting in and out of consciousness," he said. "She keeps calling your name, asking you to forgive her. Do you have any idea what she's talking about?"

Anabel frowned. "I think she knows she put the surgery off longer than she should have, and she knows I was worried about that. But she's delirious, so who can tell for sure? How soon can you operate?"

He shook his head. "She's too weak for surgery now. We'll have to build her up first. Where's her husband?"

"At work. I left him a note. Jud, isn't it risky to wait?"

"It would be riskier to take her to surgery in her present condition. Come on, let's go find some coffee. The nurses are putting her to bed. One of the residents will stay with her until I return."

At that moment Bill Tremaine burst from the elevator and, seeing them, ran forward. "Where's Lucy? Is she all right?"

Jud began talking in a quiet, reassuring voice,

describing Lucy's condition. Anabel could actually see Bill beginning to calm down as Jud talked.

By the time Jud finished, Bill was composed but bewildered. "I had no idea it was so serious. I didn't know Osborne had recommended surgery. I didn't even know she'd seen you, Dr. Westby."

"She didn't want to worry you," Anabel said.

"Was she just going to let herself die to keep from worrying me?" Bill asked angrily.

"She should have had surgery months ago," Jud said. "Apparently she developed an irrational fear of it, which she dealt with by refusing to accept the seriousness of her condition. It's a classic reaction."

"Well, she'll have surgery now, as soon as you think she's strong enough," Bill vowed. "I'll talk to her. I'll get her to agree."

Later, after Lucy's condition had stabilized and Jud felt he could safely leave the hospital for a few hours, he found Anabel in the nearest waiting room. Knees drawn up, she sat sideways in an armchair, her cheek against its back, dozing.

Jud touched her gently. "Anabel."

She was awake instantly, her eyes wide. "What is it? Nothing's happened to Lucy, has it?"

He pulled her to her feet and held her in a comforting embrace. "She's stabilized. All we can do now is try to build her up and wait. Come on, I'll take you home."

Anabel felt as though she'd worked a week of twenty-four-hour days. Nothing was more exhausting than worrying and waiting and wondering. She realized she was leaning on Jud, that she never wanted him to let her go. Drawing a bracing breath, she stepped out of his arms. "I have my car."

"Which you're in no condition to drive. You can worry about your car later. I'm driving you." It sounded very much like an ultimatum, and she was too tired to argue.

In Jud's Mercedes Anabel put her head back and closed her eyes. She felt totally drained, and she was still so worried about Lucy. Why hadn't she talked her into having the surgery sooner? Or at least talked to Bill about it? She should have realized that Lucy's adamant refusal was rooted in fear and therefore not a rational decision. She should have been begging Lucy for forgiveness, not the other way around. She still wasn't sure what Lucy had been asking to be forgiven for. Did it mean she'd given up, that she was convinced she would die? Was she asking Anabel to forgive her in advance for dying?

Jud's hand trapped Anabel's restless fingers. "If anyone can save her, I can, and I will, Anabel. If it's humanly possible."

Strangely it didn't sound egotistical. It sounded like a simple statement of fact, and she believed him. She opened her eyes to gaze into his. "I know you will. I—I was just thinking . . ." Suddenly her throat tightened achingly. She hadn't realized she was so close to tears. Embarrassed, she looked away.

His hand tightened on hers. "What were you thinking, love?"

The lights of Charleston were a blur as they drove

130

through the May night. It was after midnight, and the muffled noise of an occasional car was a quiet, distant sound. She and Jud were in a separate world, in a place and a moment out of time. Anything less than complete honesty seemed superfluous.

"I was thinking," she murmured, "that everyone I love dies." And then she let her tears fall, no longer trying to stop them. She simply let them slide down her face. Even the small effort required to wipe them away seemed too much for her.

"Ah, sweetheart, come here." Jud pulled her body against his side, held her tightly with his free arm. "You have to believe Lucy will live. I believe it."

She nestled her face in the curve of his neck. "Really? You aren't just saying that?"

"Cross my heart," he said with great seriousness. "Right now you're the one I'm worried about."

She shifted and settled against him more comfortably. "I'm all right," she murmured. As long as Jud held her, she was all right, she realized, dreading the moment when they would reach her house and he would leave her.

But it seemed he had no intention of leaving. He parked in her driveway, helped her from the car, and, his arm still around her, walked her to the house. Inside, he sat her down on the couch. "Stay right there. I'll be back."

Limp with weariness, she sat without moving, and moments later she heard him rummaging around in the kitchen. He came back with a glass of red wine. "Drink it," he instructed. "Doctor's orders."

Anabel obeyed, her eyes heavy over the rim of the glass. He saw strands of pale hair that had escaped their pins framing her face, her slender fingers curling around the glass stem, her soft lips against the rim, the slight movement of her throat as she swallowed. His pleasure in simply watching her was enormous. He imagined her naked in his arms through the long hours of the night, how he would comfort her and make her forget everything but him. He thought of what his mouth and hands could do and drew in a rough breath as a shaft of desire shot through him.

She blinked at him as she finished the wine, acutely aware of his scrutiny. He took the glass from her fingers and set it aside. He looked down at her with an uncertain expression. "Better?"

Now he was going to leave. Suddenly she knew she couldn't bear it, couldn't stand the thought of being alone in the night. "What am I going to do, Jud?" she whispered.

"About what?" he asked hoarsely, the softness and vulnerability of her constricting his throat.

"You." Her eyes were wide and a little sad and completely candid.

He reached out for her in slow motion, giving her time to draw back, and she let him pull her to her feet and hold her against him without a sound of protest. "What do you want to do about me?" he grated hoarsely in her ear.

Her soft moan had a familiar sound; it was the same moan she had uttered in her dreams of Jud these past

132

few weeks and in her waking loneliness as she wandered around her house at night. "I don't know, but . . . please don't leave me alone."

Happiness surged within him. "I've no intention of leaving you," he rumbled, and lifted her from the floor, swinging her up in his arms.

Her bed lay in a pool of moonlight, and Jud set her there in the center of the silver circle. He thought he must be dreaming. In the soft light she looked ethereal, a vision too lovely to be real. His hand moved to cup her head and, mute, he stared down at her for a moment. Then his fingers began trying to undo her hair.

"Let me," she said softly, lifting deft hands to unpin and unbraid. Then she shook her head, and the moon-gilded tresses slid over her shoulders and down her back like swatches of the finest silk.

He bent over her slowly, as though in a dream, and covered her mouth with his own. She tasted of wine and feminine sweetness. His breath escaped in a moan as his knee came down on the bed beside her. When at last he lifted his head and looked down into her eyes, she swallowed convulsively and released a shaky breath. "Wait," she whispered, lifting a hand to caress the faint roughness of his cheek. Her hand slid down to cup the side of his neck, and the touch of her flesh against his was so erotic, she began to shiver. She closed her eyes and swallowed again. "Wait," she gasped, as though she had forgotten how to breathe.

She began to undress, and as her garments were peeled away, exposing bare flesh, he kissed her throat, the protrusion of her collarbone, the curve of her shoulder as if the taste of her were nourishment and he a starving man.

At length she knelt on the bed before him, naked. She was even more beautiful than he remembered. With an impatience so huge, he thought it would tear him apart, he stripped off his clothes. He wrapped his arms around her tightly, pressing her breasts against him, and they fell prone on the bed.

"Anabel," he whispered hoarsely, "God, Anabel, I ache for you." His mouth moved over her skin, hot and seeking, leaving a path of fire in its wake.

She moaned helplessly, and her body arched into the masculine curve of his. For an instant panic and desire beat together in her as she struggled to understand what was happening. They had been downstairs, and Jud had brought her wine to drink. He had held her in his arms while she pleaded with him not to leave her alone. Then he had carried her upstairs and deposited her in this enchanted pool of moonlight. And suddenly there was no one in the world of any importance but Jud; there was nothing but the feel of his body against hers and the sensual sting of his hot mouth on her skin. Desire overcame panic, and she held his head in her hands and urged his mouth back to hers.

The taste of him was heady, like the finest French champagne. Their soft moans and labored breathing became a part of the enchantment surrounding them. When at last he raised his head and looked into her face again, his eyes were black and hungry and desperate, and the need in them made her tremble and cry out, "Jud! Oh, Jud . . ."

Her breath shuddered between her parted lips as his hot, wet mouth closed over one hard and straining nipple. "Anabel . . ." His hot breath fanned over the sensitive skin of her breast. "I can't wait any longer."

Her hands stroked the taut muscles of his shoulders before burying themselves in the hair at the back of his head. "I don't want you to wait."

His arms tightened almost fiercely on her as he entered her, and she was drowning in a sea of passion. "I love you, Anabel," he gasped, and she lifted her body to meet him. His strong hands cradled her hips, and he took her mouth in a desperate kiss, his tongue finding hers.

Jud had waited eight long years for this moment. Passion was like an unleashed beast in him, raging, rising higher and higher. Anabel moved against him with the same convulsive need that she could no more restrain than he.

Dazed, she thought, *I love him.* But even as she gave herself to him, she couldn't say the words. Vaguely she understood that she held that tiny part back for Tim. And then she could understand nothing but her need for completion, the blazing heat in the deepest core of her. She closed her eyes as the wild climb of passion reached its zenith and exploded and shuddered through her. She uttered a desperate

135

and incoherent sound because she could not say she loved him.

Jud surged against her and cried her name again and again, like one who chants a prayer.

136

CHAPTER EIGHT

During the night Jud reluctantly extricated himself from the warm pliancy of her body to go back to the hospital. Dressed, he stood beside the bed, peering down at her in the predawn grayness. She slept with her legs slightly flexed beneath the bedclothes, one arm slung across the pillow he had used, her face half-hidden by tousled blond hair.

She had cried after they'd made love, her tears rending the fabric of his heart. Confused, he had held her, whispering, "I'm sorry. I didn't mean to hurt you. Shh, love, don't cry."

Finally, her tears subsiding, she'd murmured, "You didn't hurt me," and, nestled against him, had fallen asleep. He had lain in the darkness, dismayed, his arms wrapped around her, feeling the even rise and fall of her breasts against his side. Too late, he realized her body had wanted him but not her mind. He had never meant to pressure her into intimacy before she was ready, but tonight events had conspired to make him forget his good intentions.

Spreading his hand over the feminine roundness of

her hip, he whispered, "Oh, Anabel, what have I done to you?"

He had finally slept for a couple of hours, awaking to stare into the darkness for a few moments before he could orient himself. Touching the tempting mound of Anabel's breast, he had fought a desperate battle with himself to keep from waking her and making love to her again. She had stirred, mumbled softly in her sleep, and gone on sleeping.

Now he looked down at her, terrified that he had breached her defenses too soon. He stifled an impotent sigh and slipped from the room, returning briefly a few minutes later to lay the note he'd written on the bedside table.

The early-morning sunlight falling on Anabel's face woke her. It was a moment before she remembered what had happened last night and turned on her side, expecting to find Jud sleeping beside her. When she saw that she was alone in the bed, a flood of mingled relief and regret washed through her.

Then she saw the note anchored by a ring of keys on the bedside table. "Maybe I should wish last night hadn't happened, but I don't," Jud had written. "I love you more than I can say. I've gone back to the hospital to check on Lucy. I took a taxi and left you the car. J."

Tears welled in Anabel's eyes. She couldn't honestly wish last night hadn't happened, either, and that filled her with guilt. Her love for Jud was a betrayal of Tim's memory. Yet, even with Tim between them, it had survived eight years of separation. She had no idea how to deal with such an impossible dilemma.

At the moment her worry over Lucy took precedence over her personal problems. She showered, dressed, ate a piece of toast with her coffee, and was at the hospital within an hour of rising.

She was able to get colleagues to take her surgery schedule for a few days and split her time between her office and Lucy's bedside. She didn't know how she would behave with Jud until she ran into him in the hallway outside Lucy's room Tuesday afternoon.

"Thank you for leaving the car for me," she said. She fished in her purse for the ring of keys and handed it to him.

Jud pocketed the keys, studying her. He might have believed her to be cool and collected if he hadn't noticed the pulse beating rapidly at the base of her throat. "Are you all right, Anabel?"

All at once she was assailed by every doubt she'd ever had concerning Jud. For an instant she tried to tell herself that Jud had taken advantage of her emotional state the night before. But it wasn't true. She had been a willing partner in her own downfall. Now their relationship was infinitely more complicated than before, and she wasn't ready to cope with her feelings for Jud yet.

"Of course," she said distantly, refusing to meet his penetrating gaze. "How's Lucy?"

"Stable. She's sleeping now."

"I'll just go and sit beside her bed for a few minutes."

She left him without a backward glance, and Jud clenched his hands into fists to keep from grabbing her and forcing her to look at him and really talk to him.

For the rest of the week, at night and during odd moments at the hospital, Jud tortured himself with memories of Anabel's coolness. After Monday night she put a distance between them that he couldn't cross, no matter how hard he tried. When she wasn't working, she was at Lucy's bedside. The only evidence that she went home at all during the week was the fact that she appeared each day in different garments. Unable to get more than the barest civilities out of her at the hospital, Jud had gone to the phone a dozen times at night to call her at home. But each time he'd thought better of it. Between work and her worry over Lucy, Anabel was worn-out, her nerves frayed. It wasn't a propitious time to try to talk to her about them.

Toward the end of the week Lucy's condition began to improve, and Jud tentatively scheduled her for surgery the next Tuesday. The close vigil he'd kept over Lucy, along with the week's surgeries and office appointments, had exhausted him. He knew he needed to rest during the weekend, but all week he'd dreaded wandering around his rented house alone. He decided he could safely leave Lucy Tremaine in the care of a colleague for a couple of days and made plans to go to Hilton Head Island. It was close enough that he could be back in Charleston quickly if anything came up. Friday evening, he threw a bag into the Mercedes and drove away.

He couldn't be sure at what instant he'd decided to take Anabel with him. Perhaps the intention had been there all along. Without giving himself time to think about the fact that he might only make the situation worse, he made a stop at a shopping center, then drove to her house.

Anabel had been home about an hour, long enough to get comfortable in slacks and a loose-fitting tunic, her feet thrust into a pair of low-heeled sandals. She'd removed the lingering traces of her makeup and had taken her hair down, brushed it, and fastened it in a clasp at the nape of her neck. She thought that for the first time all week she'd be able to get a good night's sleep. Lucy was doing well, and Jud had apparently decided to leave Anabel alone for the time being; Anabel's tension of the past week had subsided.

Then she opened the door, and there was Jud. Without thinking she blurted, "What are you doing here?"

His chuckle sounded weary. "The question is how have I stayed away this long."

Anabel felt an odd tweak of pleasure that was difficult to deny. She frowned, not quite sure what to say. "I-I'm sorry I can't invite you in. I'm very tired and plan to go to bed early."

He leaned a shoulder against the door frame and looked down at her with a pensive expression. "Come for a drive with me first. It'll help you relax."

Relax? With Jud by her side—hardly. But the idea of driving leisurely around the city at night appealed to her. What harm was there in spending half an hour with Jud? She hesitated, wondering if she was about to make a big mistake. "All right. Let me get a sweater, in case."

"You won't need a sweater, love," Jud muttered to himself. He wandered off the porch and glanced idly down the quiet street, which wound between stately old houses. He hoped he wasn't doing something stupid. But he didn't know what else to do; Anabel's unapproachable manner during the week had defeated him at every turn. She came out on the porch, locked the door, and ran lightly down the steps, her shoulder bag swinging, trailing a sweater in one hand.

"I guess I don't need this, after all," she said as she got into the car and tossed the sweater into the backseat. "Don't let me forget it when you bring me back."

Jud was quiet as he drove south through town. They connected with the interstate, and still Jud did not turn back. Anabel shot him a look. "Where are we going?"

Jud seemed completely at ease in the seat beside her, one hand hanging idly over the top of the steering wheel. "You'll see." He met her cautious stare equably.

Anabel looked at him for a moment, then settled comfortably in the leather seat. "Okay, keep it a secret if it pleases you."

He chuckled. "It does please me. Why don't you just sit back and relax. I'll tell you when we get there."

Suspecting nothing, Anabel sighed and, lulled by the smooth motion of the powerful car, closed her eyes. She was so tired, and cruising along the highway in the Mercedes was like being rocked in a cradle. Within seconds she was dozing, her head lolling to one side until Jud guided it to rest against his shoulder.

Later Anabel awoke when the car slowed and turned off the interstate. With a frown she straightened and looked out the window, searching for familiar landmarks. From what she could see in the car lights, they were on a narrow road, but the occasional building she saw along the edge of the road was unfamiliar.

Frowning, she checked the illuminated dash clock and gasped. They'd been driving for almost an hour. "Jud, is that clock right?"

"Pretty close."

She pressed nearer to the window. "Where are we? This doesn't look like any part of Charleston I've ever seen."

They turned into a long, tree-lined road with what looked like two-story apartments on both sides. "We're not in Charleston," he responded with a trace of defensiveness in his voice. He brought the car to a stop in front of a sprawling lighted building from which winding graveled paths led to the other buildings in the complex. "This is Hilton Head Island. I've reserved a beach condo for the weekend."

"You've *what!*"

He unbuckled his seat belt. "I knew I'd never get you to come with me if I told you where we were going."

"So you kidnapped me?" she sputtered. "Well, you can turn right around and take me back to Charleston!"

He heaved a sigh. "It's late, Anabel, and I'm too tired to make that drive again without some sleep." Ignoring her dagger-eyed stare, he got out of the car and went to check in. Anabel sat there, fuming, considering going in and trying to rent a separate condo. But she knew there would be no available accommodations on a Friday night late in May. For an insane instant she considered getting out of the car and walking back to the highway to hitch a ride home. But angry as she was, she wasn't mad enough to do anything so dangerous. She could kill Jud for this! She didn't even have a toothbrush, for God's sake.

When Jud came back with the key, she sat rigid in the seat beside him while he drove to one of the beachside condos. He went around the car and opened the door for her. "Come on, Anabel. You can sulk inside as well as out here."

"Sulk!" she echoed, scrambling out of the car. "What did you expect, that I'd throw myself into your arms in gratitude?"

Jud strode ahead of her down the path. "I did hope you might appreciate a short vacation," he said as he opened the door. He went inside and began turning on lights.

Anabel followed in stony silence. The room in which they stood was dominated by one entire wall of large, tan stones with a floor-level fireplace at its center. The wall overlooking the beach, from which the sound of the surf could be heard, was all glass, rising to a peak that disappeared into the rafters of a cathedral ceiling. A long, low, champagne-colored sofa piled with fat, earth-tone pillows was positioned at right angles to the fireplace facing two armless chairs upholstered in plush velvet of a rich bronze color. Between the sofa and chairs, a geometrically patterned rug in ecru and brown and deep aqua defined the cozy conversation area. Beyond the sofa, the gleaming flagstone floor stretched into a fully equipped, compact kitchen separated from the main room by a wood-paneled bar. It must cost a fortune to rent this place for a weekend during the season, Anabel thought.

Turning on Jud, she said, "I'm resigned to staying here until morning. How many bedrooms are there?"

"One." His tone was pleased, she noted.

"You take it, then," she said abruptly, "and I'll sleep on the sofa." She plopped down in a chair and stared at the cold fireplace.

"I bought a few things I thought you'd need." When she didn't even look at him, he went on, "I'll leave them in the bathroom off the hall and use the other bath." He hesitated another moment, seeing

145

the stiffness of her back, and a grin tugged at his mouth. Intuitively he knew her anger had more to do with saving face than with offense. They had crossed a boundary last Monday night, and there was no going back. The only way open to them now was straight ahead. He had little doubt about what the outcome of this night would be. He had no intention of sleeping in that big bed alone.

In the elegant chocolate-and-gold bathroom Anabel found a paper sack containing a fairly complete assortment of feminine toiletries. There was even a man's pajama top pulled through one of the circular gold towel racks. Jud had thought of everything, damn him.

Since she was stuck there for the time being, she might as well enjoy the facilities, she told herself, eyeing the generous proportions of the sunken tub. She turned on the water, undressed quickly, and, with a tired sigh, slipped into the tub until only her head and shoulders were above the water line. She stayed there for almost half an hour, giving Jud plenty of time to shower and go to bed.

After brushing her teeth with the new toothbrush and dusting herself generously with the lilac bath powder that she found in the sack, she put on the blue pajama top. It fell to mid-thigh. She rolled the sleeves up to her wrists and inspected the contents of the linen closet in the bathroom. A few minutes later, carrying pillow, sheets, and a light blanket, she stepped into the hall.

She released the breath she had been holding upon

finding the main room unoccupied. All the lights were turned out, except for a frosted globe hanging on a heavy brass chain in one corner. Jud must have gone to bed. She spread the sheets and blanket on the sofa, propping the pillow against one of its arms.

Straightening, she turned around and gasped when she found Jud standing behind her wearing the pajama bottoms that matched the top she wore.

"Jud!" Anabel brought both palms to her hot cheeks and took a deep breath. "You scared me to death! I thought you'd gone to bed."

He looked at her with great tenderness but didn't move. "I love you, Anabel."

She stared at him, and her trembling hands fell to her sides. Why must he persist in telling her that? It made it so difficult for her to think intelligently. She kept her voice calm as she stooped to fold back the blanket and top sheet. "I wish you wouldn't say that, Jud."

He frowned at her slender form in the oversize pajama top, half turned away from him. Her bare toes dug into the thick pile of the rug, the ivory beauty of her long, shapely legs sending a quiver through him. Her seeming casualness made him suddenly angry. "Tough! Is the truth so scary, Anabel? Why can't you accept it? We belong together."

She straightened again, her eyes widening as she faced him. It was not easy to hang on to her composure with Jud standing there, bare to the waist, his dark eyes flashing with anger. "No, you're wrong. We have no future together. Too much has happened."

The tension gripping her spine made her want to scream. "I'm not angry anymore about the underhanded way you got me here, but it doesn't change anything."

"Don't be so fatalistic, dammit! I said I love you, Anabel." He was almost shouting, and Anabel's eyes grew even wider, became eloquent with pleading.

"Jud, please don't—" She broke off as his jaw clenched and his eyes flared.

"Don't what?" he demanded. "Don't make you face the truth about yourself? That you're so damned stubborn or sick or something that you're harboring an eight-year-old resentment and want to waste the rest of your life keeping it alive!" He grabbed her by the shoulders and shook her. "We belong together. There's not a shadow of a doubt in my mind about that, after last Monday night. Why won't you let go of the past?"

"Jud—"

"Shut up," he commanded. He jerked her close and kissed her. She felt the desperation, the temper in the tense arms that clamped her body against his and in the hot frustration of his mouth. When at last he lifted his head, he didn't loosen his grip one iota. "If we can't have a future, I'll settle for a weekend," he said in a rough voice, and brought his mouth down on hers again, hard and insistent. But even as he made the capitulation, he knew he didn't mean it. His life would be dust without her to share it. His hands slipped beneath the pajama top, cupped her bare bottom, and hauled her closer. He broke the kiss, and his eyes blazed with dark fire. "I need you, Anabel, so much. Let us have this weekend."

"Jud . . ." She was breathless, dizzy. This place, this night, the feel of Jud's hard, aroused body pressing insistently against hers were like a dream from which she never wanted to awaken. She longed to shut out everything else, forget they had a life outside these walls. Why couldn't she let herself live the dream for one weekend? Her eyes misted over. "Oh, Jud!" Convulsively she wrapped her arms around his neck. "I need this weekend too." She brought her palms to his cheeks, framing his handsomely chiseled face. She looked deeply into his eyes. "I want you, Jud."

Seeking and urgent, their lips came together. Their mouths tasted and probed and clung. When he broke the kiss briefly to sweep her up in his arms, she murmured a soft, but insistent, protest, her mouth seeking to taste more of him as she pressed a kiss to the curve of his neck. She uttered a little moan of satisfaction as he carried her into the bedroom.

"What a nice big bed," she whispered.

"Mmmm." He grinned at her in the moonlight as he lowered her to lie on the cool, satin coverlet and sank beside her. "Exactly the right size." He slipped his hand beneath the pajama top to feel her skin.

"The right size?" Anabel smiled into his eyes, running her fingers along the bone-hard muscles of his shoulders. It had to be a dream, she thought, kissing his chin and then his jaw, and she hoped she didn't wake up for ages and ages. "The right size for what, Doctor?"

"For my examination," Jud responded, catching her teasing mood. He nipped playfully at her neck. "My very thorough examination."

"The doctor always knows best," she murmured happily. "I'm only a helpless patient at the mercy of my physician. I'm in your hands, Dr. Westby."

"Hmmm, you certainly are." His tongue explored the base of her throat while his hand roamed to her breast.

"Such nice hands, Doctor." She sighed, concentrating on her own hands as they journeyed up his back and down again. "I love your bedside manner."

"I aim to please, ma'am," he murmured. "Pleasing you is my main goal in life." He unbuttoned the pajama top and pushed it from her shoulders. He trailed his lips over her shoulder and down until he found her breast.

"It is?" Her voice quivered as he drew a taut nipple into his mouth. "Honestly?"

"Swear by the Hippocratic Oath."

"Mmmm, that sounds serious."

"Yeah, serious. Would you like me to show you?"

"Oh, yes," she whispered, and urged his mouth back to hers. "I'd like that very much." Her fingers insinuated themselves beneath the elastic waistband of his pajama bottoms. When her fingers curled around him, she felt him suck in air. He moaned her name and crushed her beneath him.

She shifted, twisting so that her body straddled his.

She buried her mouth in the angle of his neck and pressed her lips against his hammering pulse.

"Anabel." His voice was low and husky. "God, Anabel, you're driving me crazy."

"That's nice," she muttered, smiling at the effect she was having on him. Slowly she pulled his pajamas down, feeling the heating of his skin as she worked his legs free. Tossing the pajamas aside, she began journeying back up his body, kissing and tasting. She felt the rippling shudders of his hot skin.

"Anabel!" With an agonized groan he gripped her waist and lifted her, joining his body to hers in one smooth, liquid movement.

She gasped, then forgot to breathe for a long moment. She was suddenly trembling with need. Her hair tumbled forward to drape her breasts as they began to move together. She could feel his fingers on her hips tightening as his passion built and the rhythm gathered momentum.

All at once her bones turned to water, and she slumped against him. Her mouth was on his, plundering and being plundered.

"You're so good . . . so wonderful." Dazed, she lifted her head only enough to look into the passion-glazed depths of his eyes. "You give me such pleasure."

His need built swiftly to explosive proportions. "Oh, love . . . love." She gave a sharp cry of pleasure as their bodies climbed the crest together in perfect harmony, like one body. No longer able to hold her head up, Anabel lay prone and shuddering atop him. A guttural sound of release was wrenched from him, and he wrapped his arms around her to hold her close as they receded from the apex of sensation, flowing into drowsy contentment.

Damp and tangled with him, Anabel lay and listened to the hypnotic surge and ebb of the ocean. She sighed contentedly. "Jud," she murmured, loving the sound of his name on her lips.

"Hmmm?" His voice sounded slurred. The fingers buried in her hair relaxed.

"It was never like this with anyone else." Her words were blurred around the edges with sleepiness.

"Not even with Kelsey?"

She amazed him by laughing drowsily. "I told you Mason is only a friend. The one time he kissed me, it just embarrassed us both."

"Good," he said with a sigh.

When she disentangled her body from his and slid beneath the comforter, he came after her and pulled her back against him, spoon-fashion. Sighing tranquilly, she settled into the warmth of him and fell into a deep sleep.

CHAPTER NINE

The dream came to Anabel again during the night. Later she wondered if it was triggered by the steady drum of rain against the roof or the distant growl of thunder or the wreck of her emotional defenses wrought by Jud's lovemaking. Against the dark landscape of sleep, she made that terrifying drive to the hospital with Tim beside her, assured him he would be all right, saw him die before her eyes, heard his final accusation, "You promised, Anabel!" In the nightmarish grip of guilt and despair, she moaned and thrashed, struggling to force Tim back from death. Then a flash of lightning bathed the room in glaring white. Anabel shot up in bed, sobbing.

In an instant the room was dark again. Jud struggled free of the twisted bedclothes and reached for her. "Anabel. It's only a dream, sweetheart. It's okay."

With a terrified lunge she grabbed him and clung. She buried her wet face against his shoulder, her arms clenched around his neck. Her flesh was cold and clammy, and she was in the grip of uncontrollable tremors. Jud untangled the bedclothes and pulled the comforter over her; he eased her down on her back and sheltered her in his arms. "Shh, don't cry, darling. You're all right. I'm here." Gently he dried her tears with a corner of the sheet. Continuing to murmur soothing assurances, he stroked her hair and rubbed his hands over her arms and back to warm and comfort her.

She pressed her face into the haven of his neck. "Don't let me go." Her tremors were easing. "Please, just hold me."

Jud swaddled her with his body, became her fortress against the terrors of her nightmare. He calmed her with whispers and stroking until, finally, she lay quiet in his arms. Her breathing slowed, became deep and even. "Oh, Jud, I'm so glad you're here. I was so frightened."

He planted tender kisses on her brow. "Nightmares can seem so real." She shuddered, and he drew her closer. "Can you tell me about it?"

"I was driving Tim to the hospital," she murmured. The dream was still very near, and she sensed that reducing it to words would push it back into the realm of unreality. "It must have been the rain that triggered it. It was raining that night too."

"I remember," he whispered, but if she heard him, she gave no sign.

She went on talking, the words falling over each other in a rush. "But in the dream the rain is a deluge. I can't see through the windshield, and I'm dodging other cars and Tim is"—she turned her head into his shoulder—"groaning and groaning. I know it's his appendix. I tell him we'll get Nesbett, he'll be all right."

Her voice caught, and she had to swallow hard to steady it. Outside, the thunder of the rain on the roof mingled with the swell of the ocean in a wild crescendo.

"I miss the hospital turnoff and finally get there by a roundabout route. They take Tim to surgery and then . . . then Nesbett comes in the lounge and tells me he's dead . . . and time gets mixed up. I run into the operating room, and Tim is strapped to the table, struggling for breath . . . and I'm paralyzed. . . . I thank God he's still alive. I want to give him mouth-to-mouth, but I can't move a finger . . . and he—he looks at me and says, 'You promised, Anabel!' because on the drive and again when they were taking him to surgery I promised him he'd be all right . . . and then he can't breathe anymore, and he dies."

Her voice had become a dull monotone. Her body had gone slack in his arms; she lay against him as limp and unmoving as a rag doll.

"Anabel." Jud smoothed her hair off her brow with both hands, tilting her face up so that he could look at her. It was too dark to make out anything but the suggestion of her features. "Have you had this dream before?"

She swallowed convulsively, and a tear trickled down over his thumb. He wished he could see her better, but he knew instinctively that she would retreat from him if he turned on a light. She drew a deep gulp of air into her lungs and released it in a weary sigh. Knowing Anabel, he suspected that she had had the nightmare repeatedly. He knew also that she had told few, if any, other people about it. If he hadn't been there tonight when she was so frightened, she wouldn't have told him. In so doing she had exposed her vulnerability. What was said could not be unsaid. It was too late for anything but candor. Mutely she nodded. "Right after Tim died I had it almost every night. Then less often. Tonight is only the second time I've had it in the past year."

"You didn't tell me all of it, did you? I'm in the dream too."

For a moment she didn't move. Then slowly she drew away from him and sat up in bed. The bedclothes rustled as she drew her knees up and bent to rest her chin on them. Oddly she felt almost cleansed for having told Jud about her nightmares. "Do you really want to know it all?"

He sat up too. He wanted to touch her, but she seemed to have isolated herself from him. "Yes," he said quietly, "tell me."

"In the dream," she said, drawing another long breath, "you come into the lounge with Nesbett, and there's blood dripping from your hands. I—I yell that you killed Tim before I run out of there." The unreality of the situation struck her all at once. She was confronting Jud with her nightmares, in which he played a leading role, yet she was strangely devoid of any feeling except weariness.

Jud's hands shook a little as he dragged them through his hair. "Amazing."

She turned her head to squint at him in the darkness. "What?"

"You might be describing my own nightmares."

"Jud, I—" She didn't know what to say. Words seemed so useless. Lifting her head, she brushed the residue of tears from her cheeks. Wordlessly she got out of bed, felt around on the floor for the pajama top, and put it on. Then she went into the living room, got the blanket from the sofa, and, curling into a chair, she wrapped it around her.

Jud put on the pajama bottoms and followed her. He switched on a lamp and pulled the other chair around so that he faced her. Her eyes were swollen from weeping. But he knew he had to get everything out in the open now. "Tim's death almost finished me, too, Anabel."

She looked at him with great sadness. It was unreal that she could sit there with him, look at him, and feel no anger or resentment. It had happened such a long time ago. "I never thought it was easy for you," she whispered.

Jud rubbed his hands over his face, and when he looked up at her again, his eyes were filled with pain. "It was sheer hell. When I left Charleston, I didn't know where I was going. But I was carrying around a terrific load of guilt, and you wouldn't even talk to me. I just couldn't go on that way any longer. I thought, if I had to see you look at me with that accusing stare one more time, I'd lose my grip completely. I ran away. I can say it now, but then I told myself I was just taking some time off. After wandering around the country for weeks, I ended up in Canada and rented a cabin in the woods of northern British Columbia. It had electricity and a pump on the back porch. I lived there almost five months."

Anabel listened expressionlessly, trying to take in what he was saying. She had wondered many times where he went when he left Charleston, but she'd never imagined him living in a forest cabin without indoor plumbing. "What did you do there?"

His lips twisted in a smile that didn't touch his eyes. "Walked miles every day. And cut wood. The cabin was heated by a wood stove, and cutting wood passed a lot of time and made me tired enough to sleep at night. But I had nightmares about Tim's death, the same as you. Eventually I got my head together and decided to specialize in surgery. I wanted to be directly instrumental in saving lives, and every life I've saved in the past eight years has been a sort of penance for Tim. It doesn't make what happened any less a tragedy, but it's given my life some meaning."

Anabel looked away from him. Slowly she got to her feet and, the blanket wrapped around her shoulders, wandered to the black expanse of windows where rain lashed against the glass. After several moments she turned around. "How did you learn to stop blaming yourself?"

Jud stood and came to her. The grief of remembering shadowed his eyes and sharpened his features. "I don't guess I'll ever stop blaming myself completely. But I whittled the guilt down to a manageable level."

Restlessly Anabel wandered over to the cold fireplace, stood looking at the empty grate. Her breath trembled out. "How?"

Jud trailed along behind her, desperate to make her understand. "I had a few sessions with a counselor, but mostly I fought my demons alone. It wasn't easy, but I did it, and eventually the nightmares stopped." He reached out, gently turned her to face him, and brushed her hair from her cheek. "Don't you see, love, that your nightmares aren't going to stop until you've dealt with your own guilt?"

"*My* guilt?" There was hurt as well as censure in her voice.

"I didn't say it was real or warranted. Guilt feelings are mostly self-inflicted." She shook her head, but he went on. "Think about it, Anabel. Your parents died and you became totally responsible for Tim. You even told me once that you had promised your mother on her deathbed that you wouldn't let anything happen to him. The night of Tim's surgery, you assured him he'd be all right, and then he died. You couldn't keep your promises, and you've been punishing yourself ever since."

Dismayed and confused, she wandered back to the windows, leaned her forehead against the cold glass, and closed her eyes. She *had* felt a heavy responsibility for Tim. Had her deep resentment of Jud all these years been a way of hiding from her own guilt? The questions hammered in her brain, chipping away at the layers with which she had cloaked the truth. She had never really faced it before. Of course, Jud was right: She blamed herself for Tim's death. No wonder her nightmares always ended with Tim's accusing, 'You promised, Anabel!' For eight years she had been walking around with such a load of guilt, it was a wonder she could still stand upright.

"The last thing I ever said to him," she whispered so quietly, he had to strain to hear, "was that he would be all right."

Jud came to stand behind her. He placed his hands on her shoulders, and she lifted her head. Their reflections in the window stared back at them. "You said it, believing it was true. It should have been true. Ah, Anabel, I've been over that night so many times. When I was in the OR getting set up, the anesthesiologist who'd assisted in an operation in that same room just before found me and told me the oxygen outlet was leaking at the wall socket and that I'd have to use the reserve oxygen supply in the anesthetic machine. I remember checking that machine, Anabel. The oxygen tank was full, and I can still see myself flipping the switch to turn it on. Then I went into the lounge for a cup of coffee, and eventually Nesbett and the others arrived and we started. I was there when the others came in, and I'd swear nobody else touched that switch. While I was in Canada I went over and over it until I nearly drove myself crazy. I had to accept the possibility that my memory was faulty, that I turned the switch off when I was sure I had turned it on. Or I had failed to touch the switch and then blocked it out and convinced myself otherwise. I accepted the blame, and then I had to stop thinking about it and pick up the pieces and go on with my life."

His voice was filled with remorse, and she turned around and looked up at him, her face drawn with grief. "You accepted your guilt, while I've tried to deal with mine by denying it and putting all the blame on you."

"It's understandable, Anabel." He took her shoulders, but she shook her head. He refused to be put off. "Remember how Tim loved life? How he gave himself and his love so freely?"

She shut her eyes on a sigh. "Jud, don't . . ."

"I'm trying to make you see something."

She opened her eyes. They swam with tears. "What?"

"Tim wouldn't have wanted you to stop living because he died."

She moistened her lips. "I haven't done that."

"Haven't you? What kind of life have you had outside the hospital since Tim's death?"

Impatience flashed through her tears. "I haven't taken a string of lovers, if that's what you mean. It wouldn't have helped."

He held her eyes with his. "I know. I tried it. I thought I could forget you with other women, but it didn't work. That's why I pulled up stakes and came back to Charleston."

The self-exposure in the words stopped her. For a moment she could hardly breathe. "It is?"

"I was well established in Atlanta, and the hospital was certainly good to me. Why else would I come back? You're the only thing that could have brought me back."

She let out a shaky breath. "Oh, dear. I didn't know. It makes me feel . . . well, responsible."

He framed her face with his hands. "That's the last thing I want you to feel. You are no more responsible for what I do than you were for Tim's death."

She spoke hesitantly. "Intellectually I know you're right, but I can't command my feelings."

"One day at a time, sweetheart. Do you think we could forget all about guilt and blame and responsibility for the next twenty-four hours?"

His hands tightened on her arms, and his eyes were dark pools of eloquence. *Tim wouldn't have wanted you to stop living because he died.* Need feathered along her skin, and she released the blanket, letting it slide from her shoulders. This man had shared her eight-year hell. He was the only person in the world who understood. She lifted a hand to feel the night's growth of beard on his jaw. "We can try."

Jud gently caught her wrist and brought her hand to his lips. Softly he kissed the tip of each finger, then guided her hand to his chest. Taking her face in his hands again, he lowered his head and kissed her eyelids. She felt a trembling start in her stomach. Her hand was still spread against him, and her fingers contracted into his coarse black chest hair. With exquisite slowness he brought his mouth down to hers. She sighed as her lips parted.

162

He accepted the tacit invitation to deepen the kiss, and his tongue entered her mouth, not to demand or plunder but to tantalize and arouse. Burying his hands in her hair, he adjusted the tilt of her head, and the erotic forays of his tongue continued. The kiss grew moister as his fingers tangled in her hair, and his questing mouth warmed her blood with pleasurable intoxication. Rain drove against the windows, and thunder cracked. Anabel felt the jolt of it in her body, and it seemed as though the unrelenting storm outside combined with the giddiness in her blood to light a wild fire inside her.

Jud slipped his hands into the neck of her pajama top to gently caress her shoulders as his tongue investigated the texture and shape of her bottom lip. His hands left her shoulders to slide pajama buttons through their holes. Anabel felt him push the top off her shoulders and down her arms until it drifted to the floor at her feet. His mouth still clinging to hers, he rid himself of the pajama bottoms and spread his hands over the flare of her hips.

As his hands roamed up the curve of her back and slowly down again, she swayed against him. "Jud, the bed . . ." The faint words died inside her mouth.

"Too far." His hands gripped her waist and, lifting her feet from the floor, he took two steps. Dazed, she sank into the sofa, and Jud followed her, his naked body half covering hers. The heat and weight of him sent a fresh jolt of electricity through her.

"Oh, Jud . . . yes."

His strong, healing hands caressed her, stroking

with exquisite sensitivity to every nuance of her response. Her body felt heavy and she stretched languidly beneath him. His mouth wandered to her throat, his lips pressing, his tongue tasting and sending shivers of pleasure along her skin. Slowly he moved lower to accept the irresistible invitation of one swelling breast. His lips brushed the silken curve with kisses, moving closer and closer to the engorged nipple. When his mouth arrived at its destination, his tongue stroked with feather lightness. Anabel moaned and arched against him as fire burst in the pit of her stomach and rippled between her thighs. Moving restlessly, she grasped his head in both hands, digging her fingers into his hair, and pressed him closer.

Her mind whirled, vaguely registering the drumming of the rain on the roof, the blackness of the stormy night beyond the windows, the warm glow of lamplight, the way the sheet-draped sofa molded to her back, the warm weight of Jud's body pressing her down. But all of this was but a dim background to the sensations in the forefront of her mind—the breathtaking brush of Jud's mouth on her skin and the caress of his fingers on her inner thigh. The distant rumble of thunder and the rhythmic pelting of the rain seemed to enclose them in an intensely private world of mindless pleasure.

"Anabel, my sweet love," Jud muttered.

She murmured a thick, incoherent response, and then her breath lay trapped in her throat as his fingers slid deeper between her thighs. She released her breath in a ragged expulsion of air and, suddenly overwhelmed by the fiercest of needs, turned her head in search of his mouth. Winding her arms tightly about his waist, she explored his mouth in desperate hunger. Her breasts were crushed between them, the coarse hair of his chest abrading her skin.

His fingers moved to the most intimate core of her, and she writhed against him, her need for him growing by fierce leaps. Matching her movements to the rhythm of his fingers, she gasped, "I want all of you . . . now."

The joining of their bodies was accomplished with one slow, moist, velvet-smooth stroke. She felt Jud's restraints giving way as a shudder passed through his body and a leisurely pace was forgotten. He increased the tempo, and his breathing became ragged as his mouth and hands moved restlessly to seek out the secret niches of her mouth, her ears, her neck.

Her world had shrunk to include only him. Enclosing him with her arms and legs, she gave herself to him without restraint. Such acute rapture was beyond imagining, so she did not even try to comprehend it. She let herself be carried along on a sea of passion as it rose and gathered speed until, with a cry of release, she lost herself and wave after wave of delight washed over her.

Anabel drifted through the day as through a dream. The rain stopped before dawn, and the sun rose to warm the air and dry the landscape. She bought a swimsuit in a local shop, and they played in the ocean outside the condo, coming out when they were tired, to lie on the beach and soak up the sun. By unspoken agreement they didn't talk of Lucy or the hospital. The day was a golden idyll—a fantasy of sun-bathed hours with no appointments to keep, no work to do, no clock to watch. That afternoon Anabel lay in the sun beside Jud, her eyes closed, her mind drifting in a dreamy haze.

She was almost asleep when he stirred and ran his fingers along her shoulder. She opened drowsy eyes, shading them with one hand, and found him turned on his side, studying her.

She smiled contentedly. "What are you doing?"

He tugged gently at her earlobe. "Admiring you."

She turned on her side, facing him, supporting her head with her hand. "Why not?" she said, chuckling. "I'm such a vision with this wet hair and no makeup, and sand between my fingers and toes."

"And on the end of your nose." He grinned and brushed at her nose, then let his hand fall to the angle of her neck and shoulder. He exerted a quick, gentle pressure that made her skin tingle.

She placed her free hand over his, her eyes teasing. "Some movie producer is going to come along any minute now and beg me to star in his next film."

His gaze dropped to her cleavage, exposed by the deep purple swimsuit, then came back to hers with a sparkle. "If he has any sense, he will."

"That's not exactly an objective opinion."

His hand stroked down her arm and settled in the

166

dip of her waist. "That's true. To me you're the most beautiful woman in the world."

His words made her feel light with happiness, and her color rose. "Do me a favor," she said, smiling, "don't ever let anybody fit you with glasses. I'd hate for you to be disillusioned."

He wasn't smiling now. "I'm completely serious."

"Are you?" she asked gravely.

"Uh-huh."

She sighed and laid her head down in the crook of her arm. "I can't remember ever having such a perfect day. If only it didn't have to end."

"Shh," he whispered huskily, "we're not going to think about tomorrow. We're going to enjoy today. It isn't quite perfect yet, but I'm still hoping."

She frowned. "What do you mean?"

Slowly he put his hand on her hip, his eyes deep and darkly cogent. "You haven't told me how you feel about me."

Her skin was flushed from within as well as by the sun. In her eyes he could see hesitancy and vulnerability. "After last night, do you have to ask?"

His fingers lingered at her thigh to caress. "I want to hear the words."

I love you. A simple statement of what they both knew, and yet she couldn't say it. How could she be sure that the dreamy love-haze of the weekend would last when they returned to Charleston? Had she really forgiven him, or herself? She couldn't be certain that the old anger and resentment wouldn't surface again.

167

"Not yet." She sighed. "Not until I know what I feel now isn't a temporary aberration. Give me time to work it through, Jud." She shivered as his hand made erotic circles on her thigh.

"I'll give you time," he said roughly, "but not much. I know I said I'd settle for a weekend, but I lied. There's no way I can be satisfied with less than total commitment from you. We've wasted too many years already."

His mouth came down on hers urgently, as the necessity to communicate his desperate need with more than words rose in him. Her pulse hammered, and recognizing her own need, she caught him closer.

Moments later he pulled her to her feet, and they ran to the condo to indulge their exploding passion away from prying eyes.

CHAPTER TEN

"How's our star patient?"

It was early Tuesday morning, and Anabel had come directly to Lucy's room, not stopping at her office. Lucy was scheduled for surgery at nine, and Anabel wanted to be there before the preoperative narcotic made Lucy too drowsy to be aware of her presence. Bill, looking harried and unrested, stopped her just outside and, taking her arm, led her down the hall a few steps.

"The doctors say she's strong enough physically to undergo surgery," Bill said in a low voice, "but something's wrong, Anabel."

Catching some of Bill's anxiety, Anabel frowned. "What do you mean?"

"She's troubled over something, deeply troubled. But she won't talk to me about it. I tried all weekend to get her to."

The previous afternoon, when Anabel visited Lucy, she'd gotten the impression that her friend was worried but assumed that it was fear of the surgery.

"It's not uncommon for patients to be anxious when they're facing major surgery."

Bill shook his head and said emphatically, "It's not the operation. She has the greatest confidence in Dr. Westby. Sure, she's nervous about it, but there's more to it than that. Maybe I'm overly concerned, but I've always heard how important mental attitude is, and frankly, Anabel, I'm scared stiff for Lucy to go into that operating room in her present state of mind." He gripped Anabel's arm like a man grabbing a life preserver. "I thought maybe you could talk to her, see if you can find out what's bothering her."

"I'll try," Anabel said. "The pre-op medication should help her relax. Have they given her anything yet?"

"A few minutes ago. The nurse said she'd probably be asleep by the time they came to take her to surgery."

"Do you want to come in with me?"

"I'll wait out here."

Lucy turned her head toward the door as Anabel entered. She looked as small and frightened as a child, her freckles standing out like mud splatters on her white face. She had obviously been crying. Anabel felt uneasy. Bill had not exaggerated his wife's state of mind.

Hiding her concern, Anabel smiled and took Lucy's cold hand in hers. "How's it going, Lucy?"

"You here again?" Lucy tried to smile, but it didn't quite come off. "You've spent more time in this room than working since I was admitted."

"The office will wait."

"Don't you have surgeries today?"

"I got Sam Adler to sub for me today. I'll return the favor the next time he wants to play golf all day."

"How can you be so good to me?" Lucy's eyes had taken on a faint glaze from the narcotic. Tears spilled from her eyes and trickled down the side of her face and into her hair.

Anabel got a tissue and blotted the tears. She was becoming genuinely alarmed. This maudlin self-pity —or whatever it was—was not like Lucy. "Because, you nut, I love you. I want to be here for you, the same way you'd be here for me if I was about to undergo surgery."

"You still don't know, do you?" Lucy's voice was slurred around the edges, and her eyes drifted closed.

"Know what?" Anabel asked automatically, not sure Lucy even realized what she was saying.

Lucy's eyes fluttered open, and she focused on Anabel with a clear effort. "When I asked you to forgive me, and you said you would, you didn't know what I was talking about. I guess I knew it all along." She closed her eyes for a moment, then forced them open. "I knew it couldn't be that easy. That's why I've been so restless, unable to sleep without sedatives."

What was this fixation Lucy seemed to have with forgiveness? What was Anabel supposed to forgive her for? Good Lord, the woman had saved her life when Tim died and had been her friend ever since.

There was nothing Lucy could do that could offset the past eight years. Surely she was delirious.

"I think I know what you were talking about," Anabel said finally. "You'd convinced yourself you couldn't survive surgery, and for some weird reason you got it into your brain that you needed my forgiveness for that. Well, it's a moot point now, anyway. Jud says you're strong enough to get through this. You're going to make it. You must believe that. You're a tough lady, Lucy, and Jud will need that toughness today."

"You talk about him so naturally," Lucy said, and the hint of a wistful smile touched her mouth. "Have you been seeing him outside the hospital?"

"Yes," Anabel answered faintly, then cleared her throat, deciding anything that would take Lucy's mind off herself until she fell asleep would be a help. Even if it meant exposing Anabel's most private life. "Actually, I went to Hilton Head with Jud last weekend."

The glaze over Lucy's eyes cleared briefly. "You and Jud . . . oh, I'm so glad. It's obvious you're still in love with him, but I thought I'd spoiled it for you forever."

"You spoiled it?" Anabel chuckled. "Come on, Lucy, you had nothing to do with it. That's the sedative talking. You just go to sleep now. They'll be coming to take you upstairs soon."

Lucy shook her head, struggling to stave off the numbing effect of the drug. "No, I can't go to surgery without telling you the truth."

172

Anabel reached for a fresh tissue and dried Lucy's eyes. "Will you be quiet? You can talk all you want later."

"I might not make it."

"Lucy, stop it! When you wake up in recovery, you're going to realize how silly you're being."

"I know Jud's a miracle worker, but there's always the outside chance." Lucy spoke deliberately now, forming each word with care. "In case I don't have another chance, I have to tell you now."

Anabel knew it was useless to try to reason with someone under the influence of a strong drug, so she let Lucy continue talking.

"I saw the note on the bulletin board, you see, and took it down. Jud was in the lounge, trying to rest, and I didn't think he'd even seen it. . . . He needed to rest, Anabel."

"I know," Anabel soothed, having no idea what Lucy was talking about. The only thing that was important now was to ease Lucy's befuddled mind.

"I circulated in the same OR . . . on two surgeries before Tim's."

She's mixing up the past and the present, Anabel thought, and made more soothing noises.

"We had a . . . gunshot wound right before . . . the outlet started leaking when they were closing . . ."

Anabel's hand on Lucy's forehead grew suddenly still. *The anesthesiologist found me and told me the oxygen outlet was leaking at the wall socket.*

All at once Lucy grabbed Anabel's hand with

amazing strength. "Everybody else had gone. I went back to check the OR . . . made sure the orderlies had cleaned thoroughly. I saw the anesthesiologist's note on the board. I thought I'd save Jud the trouble and switched on the reserve oxygen tank . . . or thought I switched it on. . . . I didn't even look, Anabel, I was so sure. Because I'd taken the note before Jud saw it . . ." Her head rolled back and forth on the pillow as she fought to finish before unconsciousness overcame her. Her chest heaved as sobs racked her body. "I never did anything like that before or since. I'd been on duty more than twelve hours, and maybe I was too tired to think straight. I don't know. It seemed the right thing to do. I only meant to help. But I never should have tampered with the machine without permission."

Anabel sat, frozen, feeling the blood leave her head. *I remember checking that machine, Anabel. The oxygen tank was full, and I can still see myself flipping the switch to turn it on. Then I went into the lounge. . . .*

Suddenly Anabel saw how it could have happened. The anesthesiologist had written a note to Jud, telling him to use the reserve oxygen supply because the wall outlet was leaking, and tacked it to the bulletin board outside the surgical suites, knowing Jud would see it as he entered. After leaving the note the anesthesiologist must have decided he'd better tell Jud in person—or maybe he ran into him accidentally. Somehow he'd told Jud, and Jud had gone into the operating room, checked the anesthetic machine, and turned on the oxygen. Everything was ready for Tim, but nobody else had arrived yet, so Jud went into the lounge for a cup of coffee. That must have been when Lucy came back, saw the note and Jud in the lounge. Wanting to help, but probably not as sharp as she should have been because of weariness, she'd gone into the OR and flipped the oxygen switch. Off. *Because Jud had already turned it on!*

"I should have left it up to the doctors, or at least told Jud what I'd done. I didn't know about Tim's death until the next afternoon when I came on duty. I know . . . I know I should have told somebody what I'd done." Her fingers on Anabel's were like a vise. "But I was terrified. I knew I'd lose my job, probably never work as a nurse again, but that wasn't what stopped me. I—I was afraid I'd be arrested."

Anabel extricated her hand from Lucy's grip and battled a feeling of rising hysteria that made her want to scream. Lucy had lived with this all these years. Guilt-ridden. Terrified. Above all else Anabel had to remain in control. She lifted a shaking hand and placed it on Lucy's rolling head. "Be still, Lucy."

"You can't possibly know"—Lucy's words shuddered out—"the guilt I've suffered. I did everything I could to make it up to you . . . but I knew, no matter how much I did, it would never be enough. I couldn't make myself tell you. It wouldn't help Tim . . . and you'd hate me, shut me out the way you did Jud. I know I'm a coward, but I couldn't . . . When I found out about my heart condition, it seemed only right . . . poetic justice . . . retribution for Tim's death. Now do you see why I think I might not make it?"

Anabel closed her eyes briefly. She fought back emotions that she couldn't even name. "That's nonsense, and you know it, Lucy." Her voice grew steadier as she went along. "There is no connection between the deterioration of your heart valve and Tim's death."

Lucy's head stilled, and her clenched hands relaxed against the white sheet. "Can you . . ." she whispered faintly, ". . . can you ever forgive me?"

Don't think about it now, Anabel ordered herself, you can deal with it later. She knew what she had to say, what she had to make Lucy believe before she lost consciousness.

"I forgive you, Lucy. Of course, I do."

A shudder ran through Lucy's body, and she closed her eyes. Her mouth moved slightly, but no sound came. She had passed beyond awareness.

Anabel was still sitting beside the bed as though she were in a trance when they came to take Lucy upstairs. When the nurse and orderlies appeared in the doorway, she got up slowly and went out into the hall where Bill was hovering.

"Did you have any luck finding out what was bothering her?"

Anabel evaded, "I think I was able to ease her mind a little."

"They won't let me go up with her," he said. "Would you go with her, Anabel?"

Lucy wouldn't know she was there, but it would

make Bill feel better. So she agreed. The shock of what Lucy had revealed was wearing off, and Anabel was able to think cogently again. Had she really forgiven Lucy just now, or had she simply uttered empty words? She didn't know. She only knew that she *wanted* to forgive her friend. She was so tired of trying to place blame. She was beginning to doubt that blame existed. Tim's death had been a freak accident, a tragic fluke.

She followed the gurney into the elevator and got off at the surgical floor. It was dawning on her finally that Jud had suffered wrongfully for eight years. What would he do when he knew? She watched the orderlies wheeling Lucy through the swinging doors that led to the surgical suites, and then, almost running, she went to the lounge. A dark-haired man in scrubs stood at the coffee urn, his back to the door.

"Jud?" Anabel's voice quavered with emotion. When the man turned around, she saw that it was one of the residents. "I'm sorry," she said, her hand already on the door, "I'm looking for Dr. Westby."

"I think he's scrubbing."

Jud looked up, startled, when Anabel entered the scrub room. He was leaning over one of the stainless-steel scrub sinks, his hands under the faucet stream. There was no one else in the room, but the nurses and surgical assistants would be arriving any moment.

Jud straightened up slowly and turned off the water. "Anabel? You look as though you've seen a ghost. What is it? Oh, God, Lucy isn't—"

"No," she cut him off. "Lucy's fine. They just brought her up."

They stood, staring at each other, Jud with his wet hands extended awkwardly. What on earth could she say to him? "Oh, Jud, what have I done?" She was beginning to weep now and was unaware of it.

"Sweetheart, what's happened?" He started toward her.

"You can't touch me. Your hands—"

"To hell with that. I'll scrub again." He reached for her, and she clutched at him as if she would never let him go again.

"I shouldn't be here," she whispered thickly. "People will see us."

"Forget them," Jud ordered, and brushed the hair back from her face. She had worn it loose, the way he liked it, since their return from Hilton Head. He took her shoulders and drew her back far enough to see her tear-streaked face. "Tell me what's wrong."

She pulled him close again, hanging on to his waist tightly, and rested her cheek on his shoulder. She couldn't tell him now. Besides, she had only one thing to say that mattered. "Nothing's wrong. I just had to see you—to tell you that I love you. More than my life."

"Anabel." His arms tightened around her, and he rested his face against her hair, letting the words sink in, letting the feeling of elation seep through him. "Your timing leaves something to be desired." He laughed a little shakily. He kissed her, feeling her lips tremble under his.

They heard voices, and before they could break apart, a nurse and two doctors came into the scrub room. They stopped short when they saw Anabel and Jud. Flushing, Anabel stepped out of Jud's arms. But he caught her shoulders and said in a low voice, "We'll talk later. We have a lot to discuss. A wedding date, for starters."

Smiling foolishly, she brushed past the three bystanders, who stared after her, thunderstruck.

"Oh, boy." Gretchen, back from her lunch break, appeared in the open doorway to Anabel's office. She looked much younger than her years in an orange tiered skirt and white peasant blouse, gold chains hanging from her ears and neck. "You'll never guess what Sandy told me, just now in the cafeteria."

Anabel pushed her reading glasses atop her head and gave Gretchen her full attention. She was having trouble concentrating on work, anyway. It was after one, and there had been no word from Jud or Bill. She'd just phoned upstairs and been told that Lucy was still in surgery. "Sandy? You had lunch with Leroy Sandifer?"

"We happened to be sitting at the same table. There were three other people there, too, and they all heard him." She rolled her eyes. "Honest to Pete, they talk about women being gossips. Sandy always knows the latest rumors the minute they start to make the rounds." Her eyes narrowed in speculation. "Hey, maybe he starts them. I never thought of that."

Anabel chuckled. "I doubt that Leroy has time to sit around thinking up rumors."

"Yeah . . ." Gretchen seemed unconvinced. "But he's so nosy. This one takes the cake, though. I asked him where he got his information, and he was pretty vague. Said something about overhearing some orderlies talking but wouldn't name names." She grinned wickedly. "Sandy's such a weak sister when anybody challenges him."

Anabel leaned back in her chair. She could easily imagine Gretchen pouncing on Leroy Sandifer's every word, picking apart his logic, demanding sources —needling him. Leroy had a responsible position in the hospital, and it was hardly fitting for him to be spreading gossip; but Anabel couldn't help feeling a little sorry for him. "And you get a kick out of making him squirm."

Gretchen plopped her arms on her hips. "This time he asked for it. I'm not about to let him get away with maligning one of my bosses."

Anabel sat forward, suddenly alert. "Leroy was gossiping about somebody in this office? Who?"

"You, Doc. But don't worry, I told him he was nuts."

"What on earth did he say about me?"

Gretchen slid one hip over the corner of the desk and leaned toward Anabel. "That somebody caught you and Dr. Westby in a clinch in the scrub room this morning when Westby was supposed to be scrubbing for surgery. It's not true, is it? Naw, couldn't be. I said to Sandy, 'Gimme a break, Sandy, do you really believe the two most dedicated doctors in this hospital would forget themselves to that extent? Besides,' I said, 'I happen to know Dr. Dixon has no surgeries scheduled today.' Why are you smiling?" Gretchen's voice lost its confidential tone. "Listen, Doc, this could get embarrassing for you. What if administration hears the rumor? You could be put in a position of having to defend yourself."

"I'll talk to Mason. He'll understand." But would he understand when she told him she was in love with Jud?

Gretchen eyed her perplexedly. "I can't believe you're not upset."

"Nothing to get upset about. I have a great defender in you."

"There can't be a grain of truth in it." Gretchen's expression was thoughtful. "I can't believe Westby, the surgeon's surgeon, would bring his love life into the OR."

"Highly unlikely," Anabel agreed, smiling again and watching Gretchen's expression shift as she turned the tale over and over in her mind.

Gretchen went on, as though she hadn't heard. "If he did, it must have been a nurse, lucky woman. Somebody who resembles you." She shook her head. "No, not Westby. Too unprofessional."

"On the other hand," Anabel said dryly, "even surgeons fall in love occasionally."

"With somebody besides themselves, you mean?" Gretchen grinned, watching Anabel intently. "Anything's possible." The phone rang, and Gretchen reached across Anabel's desk to answer it. "Dr. Dixon's office, Ms. Gorman speaking." She listened, and her black-penciled brows rose. She handed the phone to Anabel. "Speak of the devil," she whispered, "it's Westby himself."

Anabel took the receiver eagerly. "Jud, how did it go?"

"She's in recovery. No serious problems during the procedure."

Anabel sank back in her chair, limp with relief. "Thank God." She was peripherally aware that Gretchen hovered in the outer office, a few feet from Anabel's open door.

"I'm going to get something to eat now and check on her again." He sounded tired. "I have another surgery this afternoon." His tone deepened, became more intimate. "I just wanted to hear your voice, make sure I didn't dream what happened this morning."

Warmth flooded through Anabel. "No," she murmured, "you didn't dream it." She laughed softly. "Don't be surprised if you get some strange looks in the cafeteria, though. It seems we're a hot item."

"Already? How? Everybody who saw us was in surgery with me until just now."

"Evidently there were some orderlies in the hall outside the scrub room. One of them must have been looking when your assistant opened the door."

"Great," he said, growling. "Oh, well, it was just a matter of time, anyway. Don't let it bother you."

"It doesn't. Jud, when will I see you?"

"Not soon enough," he responded huskily. "I won't get away from the hospital until five, at least. I'll go home and clean up and come to your house about seven. If it's all right with you."

"It's wonderful. I'll be waiting."

"Anabel . . . I love you so much."

She knew Gretchen could hear her, but she didn't care. She'd already thrown caution to the wind in the scrub room earlier. Love made her forget her penchant for privacy. "I know. I love you too."

She heard his heavy intake of breath. "I want you, love. Right this minute."

Her color high, she sighed, "Me too. But I think we've shocked enough people around here for one day." She grew serious. "As you said, we have some talking to do tonight. After you hear what I have to say, you may not want me anymore."

He laughed. "Impossible. What?" He turned away from the receiver for a moment, then came back. "I'm going to lunch with Black. He's here now. I'll see you this evening, love."

She hung up, staring into space. She heard Gretchen's muffled squeal, and then the secretary thrust her head into the office. "I love it! You and Westby, making out in the scrub room. Gee, it sure makes me look like a nerd, though—the way I defended you."

"I appreciate your loyalty, Gretch." Anabel's smile was dreamy. "Now, don't you have some work to do?"

Gretchen went to her desk, laughing.

By the time Jud arrived at her house that evening, Anabel had planned and rehearsed how she would tell him about Lucy's confession. She was wearing the daffodil dress, her hair hanging, loose and shining, about her shoulders. She served one of Jud's favorite meals: lasagna; green salad with wine-and-cheese dressing; and hot, thick slices of French bread melting with butter. In short she had done everything she could think of to soften the blow.

Over dinner he described Lucy's condition, expressing satisfaction about the way she was recovering and relieving Anabel's mind on that score so that she could concentrate solely on Jud and what she had to tell him. After dinner she led him into the living room, sat him down on the sofa, and promptly forgot what she had meant to say first.

Before she could speak, he pulled her into his lap. "Anabel," he murmured, "I can't keep my hands off you another minute."

"We have to talk, Jud. Wait . . ." She searched desperately for that well-rehearsed opening sentence while his moist, intoxicating mouth found the sensitive skin beneath her earlobe. "I have something important to tell you," she finished lamely. When his lips moved down to explore the hollow at the base of her throat, she entreated, "Please, Jud."

"We have all night to talk, sweetheart." Gently he smoothed his hands down over her back.

"Jud!"

Very slowly he took his hands from her and moved his head back, in order to look into her face. He was

184

clearly puzzled by her insistence. "You're really serious, aren't you? It must be important. Go ahead."

But she couldn't sit there in his lap, looking into his eyes, so dark with love, and say what she had to say. Squirming to her feet, she wandered to the window, stared out for a moment in silence, then turned to look at him across the room. "Lucy told me something before she went to surgery this morning. I've tried all day to think of an easy way to tell you, but there isn't any easy way. That night, the night Tim died . . ."

As she talked Jud sat forward on the sofa, then came to his feet and paced the room. Her heart twisted as she watched him, but she forced herself to finish, speaking in a voice as devoid of feeling as she could make it.

"So you see," she finished finally, "it wasn't your fault. It was never your fault. I was wrong to blame you." He had turned away from her, head bowed. She couldn't keep her feelings in check any longer, and her voice shook as she continued, "I'm so sorry, Jud. I know that doesn't begin to make up for the way I treated you. I—I'd understand if you walked out of here right now—and never came back. It would kill me, but I would understand."

Jud spun around, white with anger, a despairing look in his eyes. "It could never happen like that today."

She opened her mouth but closed it again as it dawned on her that his anger was not directed at her. It was directed at himself.

"I always check the machine a second time, right before they start administering the anesthetic." He winced. "If I'd done it that night . . ." She couldn't believe he still blamed himself, after the speech he'd given her at Hilton Head: how he'd learned to live with what happened; how he'd been able to put it behind him.

Shaken by the pain in his words, she said sharply, "Jud, listen to me. . . ."

"What else is there to say, Anabel? We've pretty well covered it. Lucy shouldn't have messed with the machine, but I should have rechecked it. Period."

The finality of his tone made fear twist in her stomach. "Please."

He was quiet for a moment, then began to pace restlessly. "All right, I'll listen."

She meant to be calm, reasonable. But resentment for the years they'd wasted rose in her and made her speak fiercely. "I'm sick to death of guilt and misery and trying to figure out who was to blame. It doesn't matter anymore. Tim is dead!" He had stopped pacing and was looking at her, listening. "You've done enough penance, and so have I. God knows, Lucy has been punished enough. You know why she finally told me this morning? She was afraid she'd die in surgery, and she wanted my forgiveness. What could I say? The woman was in no mental state to undergo major surgery. I said I forgave her, and I made her believe it. But I was just numb, Jud. I didn't know if I meant it or not. Until later. Then I realized that what she had done happened eight years ago, before we

186

became friends, before I came to love her. She's the same Lucy today that she's always been. I may be slow on the uptake, Jud, but it was finally clear to me. There's nothing to forgive. It was an accident. I can't —I will not—dwell on it and live with regret any longer."

"Oh, Anabel," Jud muttered.

"When you come back to Charleston, I was so bitter. I wouldn't let anybody, except the Tremaines, get close to me. I'd just shut myself in my safe ivory tower with my recriminations and my guilt. I could hardly feel anything, and then you came back. I tried to keep on blaming you, hating you." His eyes were suddenly very dark, very direct on hers. "I didn't want to love you, Jud, but I couldn't help it. I made both our lives miserable for eight years because I couldn't let the past go, but I never stopped loving you."

He let out a quick, humorless laugh. "You could have fooled me."

She met the hurt in his eyes. "I know how I acted. The more I suspected I still loved you, the more I fought it, and you."

"I waited so long to hear you say you loved me. I thought you'd never say it, and then this morning . . . but I didn't know then about Lucy's confession. Tell me, Anabel, what if Lucy hadn't told you? Would you ever have admitted that you loved me?"

"Yes. Maybe not this morning. Not in the scrub room, probably." A shaky laugh trembled from her mouth. "But I wouldn't have been able to keep it from you much longer." She lowered her eyes for a moment, then looked back at him and said quietly, "I don't know how I could have been with you all weekend, made love with you, felt the way you make me feel, without telling you then. It can only be because I've had so much practice in suppressing my feelings. But your love forced me to stop lying to myself. I love you, Judson Westby."

He studied her with eyes made gentle by his love. "Don't you believe me?"

He came to her then, his arms drawing her against him, holding her tight. "Yes," he said thickly, his breath hot on her cheek. "I believe you."

She started to cry tears of relief and gratitude and joy. She clung to him. The harder she clung, the tighter he held her.

Finally she said, her voice muffled by his shoulder, "Promise me something."

Taking her head in his hands, he pulled her head back to see her face. She was misty-eyed and grave. "Anything."

"Promise me we'll let the past be over now. Forever."

"Ah, Anabel." He pressed his mouth to hers and tightened his hold. Long moments later he drew away, smiling, though she could still see a trace of the pain of the past eight years in his eyes. "Agreed. Now, tell me again how much you love me."

"More than anyone or anything. With all my heart."

When she wound her arms around his neck and

kissed him with softly parted lips, his mouth lingered on hers briefly. Then he lifted his head, grinning. "Now, about that wedding date. I don't believe in long engagements." Briefly his mouth touched hers, then he drew away again, waiting for her reply.

"How does this sound? We'll get married as soon as we can get the license."

He laughed deep in his throat. "Sounds fantastic."

"Good, now we can go on to more immediate concerns."

He lifted a brow. "Such as?"

Pressing her hands at the back of his head, she urged his head down. "This," she murmured, and the word mingled with his sound of pleasure as his mouth plunged her quickly, deeply into the pit of desire where all was trembling need.